She lifted her veil as she made her way toward him, and his heart slammed into his chest.

"I love you! I cannot go through with this wedding." She leaped into his arms. He instinctively placed his hands on her waist as she clung to him.

"What the..." But he didn't finish what he was going to say because she pressed her lips to his and all rational thought left his brain. His arms tightened around her and the silence of the stunned crowd matched the skip in his heartbeat.

She broke the kiss a bare second after it had begun, leaving him feeling shorted.

"Do not say a word." Her warm breath teased his ear, rousing a fire in his belly. "If you tell them you have the wrong wedding, my brothers will beat you to a pulp for kissing me. I suggest we take advantage of the surprise and run."

* * *

Running Away with the Bride
by Sophia Singh Sasson is part of the
Nights at the Mahal series.

Dear Reader,

Fear is one of the most powerful emotions we feel when we fall in love. It's often hard to trust another person not to break our heart, to let them peer into our soul and hope that they like what they see.

Divya is a traditional Indian woman who was ready to get married to a suitable Indian boy until a wedding crasher makes her realize she wants more out of life. But when she pictured her future husband, he was tall and dark, not white and sandy blond with eyes the color of the Caribbean Sea. It's about more than looks—it's about whether he can understand her culture and her family. Can he understand who she really is?

For Ethan, his heart is already in pieces and he can't trust Divya not to shatter it further. He's going to have to decide whether she's worth the risk.

I hope you enjoy this book and the pieces of my Indian heritage that I'm sharing with it.

To get free book extras, visit my website at sophiasasson.com and please follow me on BookBub, @sophiasinghsasson.

I love hearing from readers, so please find me on Twitter (@sophiasasson) or Facebook (sophiasassonauthor) or email me at Readers@SophiaSasson.com.

Enjoy!

Sophia

SOPHIA SINGH SASSON

———

RUNNING AWAY WITH
THE BRIDE

HARLEQUIN

DESIRE

HARLEQUIN®
DESIRE™

Recycling programs
for this product may
not exist in your area.

ISBN-13: 978-1-335-23267-0

Running Away with the Bride

Copyright © 2021 by Sophia Singh Sasson

All rights reserved. No part of this book may be used or reproduced in any
manner whatsoever without written permission except in the case of brief
quotations embodied in critical articles and reviews.

This is a work of fiction. Names, characters, places and incidents
are either the product of the author's imagination or are used fictitiously.
Any resemblance to actual persons, living or dead, businesses,
companies, events or locales is entirely coincidental.

This edition published by arrangement with Harlequin Books S.A.

For questions and comments about the quality of this book,
please contact us at CustomerService@Harlequin.com.

Harlequin Enterprises ULC
22 Adelaide St. West, 40th Floor
Toronto, Ontario M5H 4E3, Canada
www.Harlequin.com

Printed in U.S.A.

Sophia Singh Sasson puts her childhood habit of daydreaming to good use by writing stories that will give you hope, make you laugh, cry and possibly snort tea from your nose. She was born in Mumbai, India, and has lived in India and Canada. Currently she calls the chaos of Washington, DC, home. She's the author of the Welcome to Bellhaven and State of the Union series. She loves to read, travel to exotic locations in the name of research, bake fancy cakes, explore water sports and watch Bollywood movies. Hearing from readers makes her day. Contact her through sophiasasson.com

Books by Sophia Singh Sasson

Harlequin Desire

Nights at the Mahal

Marriage by Arrangement
Running Away with the Bride

Harlequin Heartwarming

State of the Union

The Senator's Daughter
Mending the Doctor's Heart

Welcome to Bellhaven

First Comes Marriage

Visit her Author Profile page at Harlequin.com, or sophiasasson.com, for more titles.

You can also find Sophia on Facebook, along with other Harlequin Desire authors, at Facebook.com/harlequindesireauthors!

To all those who have been afraid to go
for what they really want.

Acknowledgments

This book, and the entire Nights at the Mahal
series, would not have happened without my
awesome editor, Charles Griemsman, and my
agent, Barbara Rosenberg.

Most of all, thank you to my readers.
Your reviews, emails and letters keep me writing.

One

"**S**top this wedding!"

Ethan Connors searched the stage on the back lawn of the Mahal Hotel where a *mandap* had been set up. The couple was seated on floor-level settees under a pergola-like structure in front of a small fire. A priest dressed in loose orange clothing chanted and threw things into the fire, making it crackle and smoke.

Ethan wished he'd paid more attention to the wedding sequence the one time he'd been to an Indian wedding with Pooja. He had no idea if he'd made it in time to stop hers.

At his outcry, the bride, groom and the dozen or so people surrounding them looked at him with surprise. The priest froze and the chatter of the crowd behind Ethan died. He could feel the stares of hundreds of guests on him. He tried to catch Pooja's eyes but the heavy bridal veil covered her head and fell half-way across her face. The smoke from the fire swirled around her. He looked at the older Indian couple seated next to her. *Were they Pooja's parents?* If the glare they were shooting him was any indication, they were.

A knot twisted in his stomach. After six months of dating, including three months of living together, she'd never introduced him to her parents, and he couldn't pick them out based on the pictures he'd seen on her bookshelf.

A younger man seated next to the bride stood and made his way to Ethan. "I don't know who you are but you're interrupting my sister's wedding. You best leave quietly before I call security." The man's voice was low and icy.

But Ethan was determined he wasn't going to lose her again. He may have come to his senses in the eleventh hour, but he was going to save himself, and Pooja. She'd known the guy sitting next to her for three months. How could she marry him? *I want to know my husband and be sure that we're compatible*, she'd said to Ethan. He and Pooja were compatible. Why hadn't he seen that sooner? When she'd first brought up marriage—and how her family wouldn't approve of her relationship with a white Midwesterner unless he put a ring on her finger—he'd thought he needed more time to figure things out. But what was left to think about? He was pushing forty. His brother was ten years younger and had been married for nine years and had two kids. Pooja was the only woman who had deemed him worthy enough to even discuss marriage. He wasn't going to let her get away a second time.

Pooja was now standing, but Ethan still couldn't get a clear line of sight through the crowd that was gathering around him. He hadn't spoken to her since she walked out three months ago, but she'd sent him an email telling him she was getting married today. Why would she do that if she didn't want him to make a grand gesture? It would've been helpful if she'd sent him some details other than that her groom was planning "a grand *baarat* down the Vegas strip." He'd spent the entire morning driving up and down the strip, looking for a groom on a horse surrounded by a bunch of people dancing. The traditional Indian *baarat,* the arrival of the groom's party, would be hard to miss, or so he thought. He'd been on the other side of the strip when he'd heard on the radio that traffic was snarled because of an Indian wedding, and he'd driven like a madman to get there.

He had charged in ready to take on the world, or at least a bunch of angry relatives, but now doubt snaked its way through him. Did Pooja really want him to rescue her? And how the hell was he going to get out of the hotel without hundreds of guests and hotel security guards stopping him?

Take off your veil and look at me, Pooja. He wanted to tell her that she didn't have to succumb to her parents' pressure and marry whichever Tom, Dick or *Hari* they had found for her. He was ready to step up and make a commitment.

Another man who bore a family resemblance to the

one who'd identified himself as Pooja's brother broke through the crowd and strode toward him. Who knew how many family members there were, and Ethan had zero backup. *When will you stop being so impulsive?* His mother's familiar recrimination blared in his head.

He focused on Pooja, who was clearly looking in his direction, despite the veil on her face. "I'm sorry I was such an ass and didn't realize how much you meant to me. I want to marry you. Run away with me." Brother One whispered something into a phone, no doubt calling security. "We must go now!"

"Yo dude, this isn't some Hollywood film. What do you think you're doing?" Brother Number Two was now within punching distance and didn't seem quite as reserved as Brother One. "My sister doesn't know who you are. Get out before I..." He pulled his arm back, clearly preparing to punch Ethan in the face.

"Wait!" Pooja's voice sounded strange.

All eyes turned toward her. As she stepped down from the stage with an easy grace, she fisted some of the long burgundy skirt that flowed to her heels. It was covered with shiny gold thread and shimmering diamond jewels. The gold-colored top was cropped a few inches above her navel, showing a tantalizing strip of her stomach and back. Visions of running an ice cube across that navel, then licking up the droplets of water flashed through his mind. Why hadn't he actually done that with Pooja when they were together?

Her hands had intricate henna patterns from her fingers to her elbow, and her wrists were covered in red-and-white bangles. The crowd dispersed to let her through to him. She lifted her veil as she made her way toward him, and his heart slammed into his chest.

It wasn't Pooja.

"I love you! I cannot go through with this wedding." She leaped into his arms and crushed all the air out of his lungs. He instinctively placed his hands on her waist as she clung to him. Her skin was cool and soft beneath his fingers. She smelled like vanilla and cinnamon.

"What the…?" But he didn't finish what he was going to say because she pressed her lips to his and all rational thought left his brain. His arms tightened around her, and the silence of the stunned crowd matched his stopped heartbeat.

She broke the kiss a bare second after it had begun, leaving him feeling shorted.

"Do not say a word." Her warm breath teased his ear, rousing a fire in his belly. "If you tell them you have the wrong wedding, my brothers will beat you to a pulp for kissing me. I suggest we take advantage of the surprise and run."

She had a slightly Indian, slightly musical and entirely arousing accent. He reluctantly moved his eyes from her mouth and looked at her brothers, whose murderous expressions got him to haul ass.

"Out of our way!" He grabbed her hand. Given that there had to be hundreds of guests milling about, they had surprisingly little trouble getting moving. The guests eagerly parted so they could get a better angle for cell phone pictures and videos and then helpfully got in the way of their pursuers. It made for better social media posts if the bride actually got away.

Just wait until they find out who I am.

She matched his fast pace, despite the fact that they were on grass and she was wearing two-inch-high heels and a skirt that probably weighed more than she did. Once they got past the guests, she yanked his arm and he let her take the lead. People were shouting in various languages behind him, and he was glad he had no idea what they were saying.

Instead of running into the main building, where four men in black were making their way toward them, the bride banked a hard left. "There's a gate through the serenity garden that isn't guarded." She led them to a wooden gate embedded in a perimeter wall.

I don't think this is what they had in mind when they made this emergency exit.

It had one of those childproof locks, but she expertly handled it. Had she planned the escape route? Ethan hoped so; her brothers had recovered from their shock and were almost upon them.

They went through the gate and he pulled it shut behind him just as a hand snaked out. By the yelp he heard on the other side of the door, he'd succeeded in slamming the door shut. They exited onto a side street and he looked around to get his bearings. The front of the hotel faced the famous Vegas strip.

"Where's your car parked?" she asked urgently.

"Not far," he said and led her down the street. He had illegally parked nearby, and they had miraculously exited on the right side of the hotel, so the car was just down the block. As they approached it, he saw a ticket on the windshield. He ignored the piece of paper and went to the passenger side and touched the handle. The Tesla roadster recognized his fingerprint and unlocked. He opened the door and the bride gracefully lowered herself into the deep bucket seat. Just as he started the car, a hand smacked the passenger-side window, and he looked to see Brothers One and Two at her door. He floored the accelerator. Vegas traffic didn't really allow for a high-speed chase, so he made a series of turns, hoping to lose whoever pursued them.

"We *need* to get out of Vegas," the bride said, her voice frantic.

He drove aggressively until they were at least a mile from the hotel, then pulled into a public parking garage and stopped the car. He turned to her. Her beautiful dark eyes gazed back at him with such lustrous excitement that he momentarily lost his train of thought.

"We aren't going anywhere until you tell me who you are."

She stuck out her hand. "Divya Singh. Very nice to meet you. Now we have to get moving."

He shook his head. "*You* have to get moving. I have a wedding to crash. The right one this time."

Two

Divya resisted the urge to scream at the man sitting next to her. He didn't owe her anything, but she needed him if she was going to get away from her family. "How about I help you find the right wedding? I assume you're after an Indian bride. You'll have an easier time getting in with me by your side." The last place her brothers would look for her was at another wedding. They had no way of knowing that the man sitting next to her was a perfect stranger, and she needed his help if she was going to get to New York City. Now that she'd done the unthinkable, this was her only chance to do the one thing she needed to do.

He narrowed his eyes, and she tried not to focus on how crystal blue they were or the way that the little crinkles in the corners of his mouth sent a little tingle down her spine. He wasn't even her type. Though it was hard not to notice his sandy-brown hair, which glinted when it caught the sunlight streaming through the windows, or the angular cheekbones, sharp nose and broad shoulders. He looked effortlessly athletic and chic in a black tuxedo that looked tailor-made for him.

"Let's start with your name," she said.

He gave her a half smile and her heart gave a little kick. "Ethan Connors."

Somewhere in the recesses of her brain, the name sounded familiar, but she was sure she'd never met him before. *I wouldn't ever forget him.* She produced her best smile. "It's nice to meet you. Now, about that wedding you want to crash. What's the bride's name?"

"Pooja Chaudhry."

Divya pointed to his phone.

"I already tried googling her name and today's date and every other key word I could think of."

"Look at her social media."

"I already did."

Divya just held out her hand and raised one perfectly shaped eyebrow. He sighed, then tapped on the phone several times and finally handed it to her. Pooja's Facebook page was on the screen. She was an attractive Indian woman with straight black hair, brown eyes, a sharp nose, cheekbones to die for, skin the color of white sand and a wide mouth. Dressed in a sundress with a field of sunflowers behind her, she looked gorgeous. No wonder Ethan had fallen hard for her. Divya felt an unfamiliar twinge deep in her chest. She had no complaints about winning the genetic lottery in the looks department, so why did this woman's beauty bother her?

She clicked on Pooja's friends and began looking through their recent posts. In a few minutes, she found what she was looking for and turned the phone so Ethan could see. There was a shot of a smiling Pooja in a stunning bridal *lehnga* with the MGM Grand logo behind her.

He reversed the car and punched the accelerator. They tore through the streets of Vegas, though as much as he changed lanes, Ethan couldn't escape the slow-moving traffic on the strip. The one-mile journey took them almost twenty minutes. He finally screeched to a stop at the front of the hotel, handed the valet a key and a hundred-dollar bill. "Keep it right here, ready to go, and I'll give you a real tip when I leave."

They asked where the wedding was and were directed to one of the large ballrooms. They went inside, and as soon as she caught sight of the bride, Divya grabbed Ethan's arm. But he kept walking.

"You're too late," she said a little too loudly and cringed as a few of the guests looked in their direction. He stopped. "I'm sorry, Ethan. See how she's throwing rice onto the cloth behind her? This is done after the wedding ceremony as the bride says goodbye to her family."

Divya looked at Ethan's face, expecting it to crumple, but he sighed, and she had a feeling it was in relief and not frustration.

"I should talk to her." The way he said it, Divya wasn't sure if he'd meant it as a question.

"I believe Vegas is very liberal with their marriage annulments. If you are serious about marrying her, you should make your case."

They both studied Pooja. Like Divya, she was wearing the traditional red-and-white *choora* bangles worn by brides on their wedding day and for months to a year after, depending on the family's traditions, to signify her newlywed status. Her *lehnga* was a pink bejeweled skirt with a royal blue border and a matching top that showed off a small section of her midriff. The groom whispered something in her ear, and she smiled stunningly. She whispered something back and he laughed, then leaned over and kissed her on the cheek to the general merriment of the gathered crowd.

"It doesn't look like she wants me to save her," Ethan muttered.

Divya had to agree. The bride looked excited and happy, not teary-eyed or forlorn in any way. Not the way she herself had looked earlier this morning. A pang of jealously hit Divya. She didn't want to get married, but if she had to, she wanted to be as happy as Pooja looked with her groom.

Ethan stared at Pooja and Divya realized they were attracting a few looks. Pooja looked in their direction and Divya stepped away from Ethan.

Pooja's eyes widened. She whispered to her groom, then stepped toward them. The eyes of two hundred people followed her. "What are you doing here?" she said in a low voice once she came closer. Her eyes flicked to Divya, then back to Ethan. He stood silent.

Divya stepped up to Pooja and hugged her, then

whispered in her ear, "He crashed my wedding, looking for you." She released Pooja and said in a loud voice, "We had to come congratulate you, even though it's also my wedding day."

Pooja caught on quick. She turned around. "I need just one minute with my friend, then I'll be back."

An older lady stepped forward. "Hurry up, Pooja. The car is ready."

Pooja led the way and Divya took Ethan's hand. He frowned, and she leaned over and stood on tiptoe to whisper, "She's a married woman. Appearances are important."

He didn't argue but his lips thinned. Pooja led them through a set of doors and into a food-prep area. A waiter came toward them. "Please, just one minute," Pooja said, and he nodded.

"I'll wait outside," Divya started, but Pooja shook her head. "I need you to stay here."

Ethan shook his head. "I came here to break up your wedding and you're still worried about appearances."

Pooja glared at him. "How dare you show up here to ruin things for me? You had me, Ethan, and you let me go. If I wanted you here, I would've sent you an invitation. You're doing what you always do, going for what you want without considering how it affects everyone around you."

"If you didn't want me here, why did you send me that email saying you loved me and would've married me?"

She sighed. "Past tense, Ethan. I sent you that email for closure. It was a goodbye, not an invitation." She stepped closer and put her hand on his arm. "I said some really harsh things the last time we saw each other. I didn't want to start my new life by leaving things like that with us. I wanted you to know that you were special to me."

Ethan was silent and Divya resisted the urge to stand up for him. She looked at him, and though his eyes were focused on Pooja, he seemed to be a million miles away.

Finally he asked, "Do you want to be married to that guy?"

Pooja's eyes softened. "Yes," she said. "My parents set us up, but Anil and I fell in love."

"So quickly?" he said skeptically.

"I know you think arranged marriages are forced, but that's not the case. I was ready to settle down and so was he. We already got along with each other's families. There was no bullshit between us, so Anil and I could focus on whether we wanted to be together. It doesn't take long to fall in love once you're ready."

Pooja's eyes flicked to the door. "I'm sorry, Ethan. What you and I had was something special, but you know as well as I do that you were never going to marry me."

She gave him a chaste kiss on the cheek. "I've got to go. Try not to get in the way of your own happiness."

Ethan stood rigid with his back to the door as she left.

Divya touched his arm. "Are you okay?"

He shrugged. "Guess that's that. Where do you want me to take you?"

Divya stared at him. *How could he be so nonchalant about the woman he loved getting married to someone else?* Divya had a ton of questions for him, but he turned away from her, and she sensed that he didn't want to talk about it. Maybe he was embarrassed.

"What do you want to do next?" he asked.

Divya chewed on her lip. *Do I dare?* She'd come this far, might as well go all the way.

"There is someplace I'd like to go but…" As she said the words, the weight of what she'd done began to descend on her. She had wrestled with the decision for weeks, ever since her parents had announced her wedding to Vivek. She had protested and threatened and planned her escape, but ultimately, she'd lacked the courage to stand up to them. It wasn't until she was sitting next to Vivek by the holy marital fire that the realization hit her that she would never get a chance to love a man or be free to chart the course of her life. Nor would she get a chance to do the one thing she had dreamed of. She wasn't that religious, but in that moment, she'd prayed for an escape. And then Ethan had shown up.

"I don't have any money with me."

"You have enough jewelry on you to buy a house."

Divya's hand flew to the diamond choker around her neck. "This is my mother's. You can't sell family jewelry."

Ethan smirked. "Spoken like someone who comes from money."

Divya bristled. "You don't seem hard up. A Tesla isn't a poor man's car."

"I earn my money," Ethan said wryly.

"Well, I work, too, and if I could, I would happily live on what I earn," she said hotly, but his words burned into her. She'd been handed everything in life. While she knew how lucky and privileged she was, she had no sense of whether she was worth anything beyond her family's wealth.

She took a breath. "We don't have time to waste. I need to lay low for a few days. I don't want to face my family when they're so angry with me and while there's still a chance for them to resume the wedding. I have a bag packed with some essentials. I could call my sister and see if she could deliver it somewhere." Even as Divya said it, she knew her sister's phones and movements would be monitored by her family.

"It's probably not a good idea to contact your sister if you're trying to avoid the rest of your family. Do you have your driver's license?" He scanned her body slowly and deliberately as though he were examining her with X-ray vision.

"Hey, eyes up here." She glared at him, though little sparks of excitement coursed through her at the obvious interest in his eyes. She reached into her tight-fitting blouse and pulled out a well-worn dark blue passport with Republic of India stamped on the front.

"You're not American."

She raised an eyebrow. "Do I sound like an American?"

"Why get married in Vegas?"

"Because my fiancé—*ex-fiancé*—is American." She didn't have time for small talk, though; it wouldn't be long before her eldest brother Arjun mobilized his considerable influence to find her. "Listen, I really need to get out of Vegas. I was only able to fit this passport in my blouse. I don't have any money, but I promise you that if you can pay for a bus ticket to New York, I'll—"

He waved her off. "I'll give you whatever money you need."

"Thank you. I'll pay you back as soon as I—"

"I have more money than I can spend in my life-time. It's meaningless to me." The catch in his voice hit her in the chest.

"Is there anything I can do for you? Talk to Pooja?"

He looked at her, and she saw frustration and also a shadow of something darker in his eyes. "I think you and I both know that I've lost Pooja. Don't worry. I'm used to it. How about we focus on getting you out of town."

She wanted to know more. How could he let go of the love of his life as if he'd lost nothing more than money at a casino? *He is not my problem.* Right now she had a very short window to get away. She hadn't come to America to get married. She'd come for a taste of freedom, to do the one thing she'd never be allowed to do: to take a chance on a dream and see if she could make it come true.

"Why New York City?"

"There is something I need to do there. I'll explain later. Can you drop me at a bus stop?"

He smiled. "I have a better way to get you there. Let's go. I'll explain on the way."

Excitement exploded through her. *Can this really be happening? Am I really going to get to New York?* The idea of being able to go without the shackles of her family was incredible. She began running through the list of things she needed to do as Ethan led her out of the hotel.

They retrieved the car, which the valet had kept front and center. He handed the key card back to Ethan, who peeled off several hundred-dollar bills and handed them to the wide-eyed man.

As Divya took her seat, it hit her. *I must be mad.* Ethan was a complete stranger and she was getting in a car with him not knowing where he was taking her. What if he was a psycho or axe murderer? Why was she so at ease around him? She knew nothing about the man.

"Can I borrow your phone to check my email?"

He held the phone to his face so the facial recognition program unlocked it and gave it to her. He motored the car out of the hotel's drive-through and back into Vegas traffic. She opened up a web browser and typed his name. *Ethan Connors.* She gasped audibly as the search results displayed.

"I guess you googled me."

She looked at him guiltily. His eyes were focused on the traffic ahead, but his lips twitched.

"I'm sorry. I was curious and I just—"

"—wanted to make sure I wasn't some serial killer?"

She smiled sheepishly. "Your name sounded familiar. My family business is hotels, so I don't regularly follow the tech world, but I remember reading the headlines when your app hit one billion users and you branched into India."

He smiled. "We're at three billion globally now."

"I can't believe I didn't recognize your name. You're almost as famous as Mark Zuckerberg. Why didn't you say something?"

Ethan shrugged; his smile was shy as he focused on the road ahead. His expression sent a ping right to her heart. "Mark gets better publicity. Mine isn't so flattering."

"And why is that?"

"I'm known to be a bit of a troublemaker."

"Is that why you're helping me?"

He was silent for several seconds. "Maybe. Maybe it's because you're a nice distraction from losing my future wife."

"You hardly seem heartbroken about Pooja."

He put a hand to his chest. "And how would you know what I'm feeling?"

Had she imagined the fleeting look of relief on his face when Pooja had told him she loved her husband? *What do I know?* Divya was a basket case of emotions. Her family would be worried about her. And they didn't deserve the embarrassment and shame that would ensue in the Indian community from her running away so publicly. She should have done it before the invitations went out, or before the guests arrived, or even last night when her family could've claimed she was sick and saved face. She'd been so anxious about what it would do to them, that in the end, she'd forced herself into the worst of possible options.

She clicked through various friends' social media pages and gasped when she saw a picture of her and Ethan escaping from the wedding. As she scrolled through the feed, her heart sank even further. "There are social media hashtags about us. The one that's trending is #BrideSnatcher."

"Ha, that's clever since my company is called Deal Catcher."

Divya turned the phone off. If she read any more, her already weakening resolve would crumble further. "My parents are going to be furious. They are so careful about their media image. They're never going to forgive me."

Ethan flipped his hand dismissively. "It'll blow over in a day or two, as soon as a Hollywood celebrity announces a baby on the way or there's a new royal scandal."

It wouldn't ever blow over with her family. *What have I done?* So what if she had to marry boring Vivek? Would it be worse than being disowned by her family? He wasn't a bad guy. So what if he didn't make her heart go pitter-patter? Yes he'd laughed at her dream career, but she could've worked on him. He wasn't as traditional as her parents; she could've convinced him eventually. That was the conclusion that had driven her to step into the wedding *mandap* that morning. She mentally shook her head. *The damage was done.* There would be no point running away if she didn't do the one thing she needed to do. After that, she could return and face the music with her family. Like she always did.

Divya was so lost in her thoughts that she hadn't noticed where Ethan was driving. When he stopped the car, she realized they were at the airport. More specifically, at the private-aviation gate.

"You have your own plane?"

Of course he did. He was Ethan Connors. From the little she remembered and her quick read of his Wikipedia page, he'd started his company with an app that helped people search multiple websites for the best price on products and set an alert when items they were looking for went on sale. During the coronavirus pandemic, the app had helped people find toilet paper and other necessities and report price gouging. Since then, the app had grown into an enterprise that included an online store for exclusive products and was expanding into other areas such as real estate bargains. He'd become an overnight billionaire. Lucky for her, he wasn't an axe murderer. An adventure junkie and playboy, yes, but that she could handle.

"It's a business expense," he replied flippantly.

"And you just happened to have it ready to go?"

He smiled wistfully. "I was planning to whisk a bride away."

Her pulse jumped. *What am I doing?* Ethan had to be emotionally messed up, and here she was, taking advantage of him.

He parked the car next to a plane that looked bigger than the medium-sized Gulfstream her parents had. He exited the car, and before she had a chance to gather her skirt, he opened her door and held out his hand. *A man with manners.* She placed her hand in his and immediately felt his strength as he pulled her up. She came face-to-face with him as she stood. A warmth spread in her chest as she thought about the brief kiss she'd given him at her wedding to convince everyone that she knew him. It had been the lightest touch, but it'd felt so electric, she had pulled away fast. Now, with their faces so close, she wondered what it would be like to kiss him properly.

They stood there for several seconds, until he let go of her hand. He pointed toward the stairs leading up into the airplane.

She paused at the bottom step, the handrail hot under her hand. *This is a bad idea.* There was still time to make it right with her family. An hour had passed since she'd left her wedding. All the guests would still be there, enjoying the food and drinks her brother had likely served up in the hope that they'd find her or she'd return. If she went back, she could play it off as nerves. Her parents would be angry, but at the end of the day, the marriage to Vivek would be all that mattered. The media storm would die down. Everything would go back to normal.

But the more time passed, the more unforgiveable her actions became. There was no turning back if she stepped onto the plane.

She eyed the jet. Her entire life had been carefully mapped out. She never made a move without a plan; even an evening out required meticulous preparation.

Getting on a plane with a stranger was a recipe for disaster.

"Are you ready?" Ethan's mouth curved into a smile. Her heart stuttered. She knew what she had to do.

Three

What am I thinking? He had spent most of yesterday rehashing all the poor choices he'd made in life, and today he'd made two more spectacularly bad decisions: the first to crash Pooja's wedding, and the second to get involved with Divya's escape.

Last night he'd been at his condo in Los Angeles, unable to sleep. He barely recognized the furniture in the place, let alone remembered how to operate the overly complicated coffee machine. He owned a condo in every major city where he had to spend time for his business. He was tired of hotel rooms, yet none of these condos was home. The closest he'd come to feeling grounded was living with Pooja for three months. But when he'd been with Pooja, all he'd been able to think about was all the things that didn't work in their relationship. After she'd left, he'd been unable to stop thinking about how great things could've been between them.

He'd woken up in a cold sweat this morning, wondering whether he'd die alone in one of his ubiquitous condos. Living on his airplane, jetting from city to city was getting old. He wanted a place where he belonged; he wanted what his brother and his parents had—a soul mate. In her email, Pooja had accused him of setting an impossible standard that no woman could ever meet. Maybe she was right. He had a black book full of failed relationships. So he'd put his jet on standby and charged into Vegas, intent on getting Pooja back.

But here he was, with another woman, thinking about how her luscious pink lips had tasted of vanilla when she'd kissed him earlier. Was his mother right? Was he afraid of commitment? As he watched Divya negotiate the narrow steps of the plane in her heavy skirt, he knew it was a bad idea to spend time with her. He was attracted to her and felt the familiar urge to throw caution to the wind and pursue her like he did any endeavor that caught his attention.

"Welcome back, Mr. Connors." Kathy was one of the regular cabin attendants who worked the plane. While the jet was his, he used a contract service to provide pilots and staff. She greeted them as they entered, dressed in her regular black pantsuit, white-collared shirt and red scarf around her neck. Her graying dark hair was knotted stylishly at the nape of her neck.

"Long time no see, Kathy," he quipped.

She looked at her watch. "This isn't our fastest turnaround. I believe your record is fifteen minutes. We did get new pilots, though."

Kathy had flown with him from LA earlier in the day. If she was surprised to see Divya instead of Pooja, she kept it to herself.

He turned to Divya. "There's a bedroom in the back that has some of my clothes. Feel free to borrow something if you want to change."

Divya looked like she was going to say something, then thought better of it. While Divya was changing, Ethan discussed the flight plan with the pilots.

Divya emerged wearing one of his black T-shirts and a pair of shorts. She looked like a kid wearing a grown-up's clothes. The T-shirt swelled over her breasts, then hung down to her thighs, and his basketball shorts looked like cropped pants. She looked impossibly sexy. Her feet were bare, revealing pink-tipped toes and intricate henna patterns like she had on her hands and arms. Her black hair fell in waves over her shoulders. She'd taken off the heavy jewelry and scrubbed her face, making her look incredibly young.

Kathy closed the outside cabin door. They were in the main seating area, which consisted of several tan-leather recliner chairs, a couch with a coffee table and a mahogany-finished bar. Another door separated them from the cockpit and service area, where Kathy now disappeared. "Are we really going to New York City?"

Her voice held such longing that it wrenched his heart.

"What's so important in New York?"

A mischievous smile played on her lips. "Can I have your phone again?"

She took it, quickly typed in an address and handed it back to him, open to a webpage for Café Underground.

"It's a club that does open mic for new singers."

"You sing?"

She shrugged. "I like to sing. But I don't know if I have any talent. I sing at family events and my relatives and friends pump me with praise. I love singing. If I could do anything in life, that's what I'd want to do. But I need to know whether or not I have real talent. Just once, I want to stand in front of a real audience and see what it's like to perform live."

Her face held so much hope that all he wanted to do was make it happen for her. "You can probably find an open mic right here in Vegas. Why go all the way to New York?"

"This place is special to me." She took a breath. "When the entire world was under lockdown, Café Underground started doing these video open mics. They gave me a chance to perform, and it's the only time I've sung for someone other than my family. It went well, but it was different sitting in my bedroom, singing to a computer screen. They made me promise I'd come to do my first live performance at their club. I know it's superstitious, but I believe the place is my good luck charm. I would never have thought about a singing career if I hadn't accidently found out about their virtual open mic."

"It's a done deal. Tonight, you'll be singing at Café Underground."

She launched herself at him and gave him a hug. His arms automatically went around her waist and the feel of her took his breath away. His body went hot at the way her breasts crushed against his chest and her breath warmed his neck. "Thank you, thank you. You have no idea what this means to me."

He gently disentangled himself before his body gave him away. *What's wrong with me?* How could he go from wanting to marry Pooja to being insanely attracted to Divya? This was what he was always afraid of: that he'd turn out like his father. *Connors men have a hard time holdin' on to good.* The pattern was always the same. His father, Wade, would lose a job, his mother would work longer hours to make money for the household, and his dad would go day drinking. His mother would come home and make dinner, while his father sat in front of the TV, drinking Jim Beam until he passed out. To this day, Ethan couldn't stand the smell of whiskey. His mother had eventually left his father and married Bill. That's when Ethan had learned what an ideal marriage looked like. Bill had adopted Ethan, and his father hadn't thought twice about signing away his parental rights in exchange for never having to pay child support. Ethan wanted what his mother and Bill had, but he lived in fear of ending up like Wade.

There was a knock from the service door and the pilot stepped in, followed by Kathy.

"Sir, the operations control center is asking if we

have a Miss Divya Singh on board. Apparently her family is looking for her." The pilot looked from Ethan to Divya.

Divya's eyes widened.

"No one here by that name. This is Pooja Chaudhry, my longtime girlfriend," Ethan said firmly.

The pilot looked at Kathy, who nodded, and then he left.

Ethan mouthed a thank-you to Kathy, who smiled serenely and asked for their drink orders. He ordered a coffee and Divya asked for a glass of white wine.

Divya sank into a recliner as the jet began to taxi, and Ethan took a seat opposite her. She looked out of the window while chewing on her lip.

"Are you expecting your family to show up with guns blazing?"

She nodded. "I've snuck out of the house before, but this is a whole new level of rebellion."

"You're a grown woman. Why do you need to sneak out of the house?"

She sighed. "My family is very old-fashioned, even by Indian standards. They believe there is an etiquette that the women, the *girls* of the house as they call us, must follow."

"Pooja's family had some very strict rules on who she was allowed to date."

"If her family was even half as traditional as mine, I'm guessing a white man was at the top of the list of unsuitable boys."

He smiled. It had taken Pooja two months to tell him in polite terms that he was not what her family had in mind for her. Divya had bluntly stated it two hours after meeting him. "I was definitely not on her parents' list of eligible bachelors, that's for sure. How did you meet your fiancé?"

She rolled her eyes. "My brother set us up. *Girls* in our family don't date random men. We're set up with eligible bachelors who promise to behave themselves but, in reality, are just as wretched as a bar sleaze from the worst part of town."

"Pooja called it a global dating service." Despite the fact that they were living together, Pooja had still endured the occasional setup from her parents.

Divya nodded. "It's great for people who actually want to settle down."

"Who was the guy you were supposed to marry?"

Divya looked out the window as the jet shuddered, gathering speed in preparation for takeoff.

"Vivek. He's an NRI, a nonresident Indian as we say in India. He's a very nice guy…" She trailed off and bit her lip. "But I'm not ready to get married. To anyone. I came to Vegas two months ago to visit my brother. He set me up with Vivek and we started dating. When I went back to India, I thought our affair would fizzle out, but he proposed marriage to my family, which is the proper way of doing things. No one bothered to ask me if I really wanted it. They assumed that I was ready to get on the marriage-and-baby-making train. Arjun and Vivek planned this big Vegas wedding, and my family packed my bags so I could start my married life in America."

"What's wrong with marriage and babies?"

"Nothing. If that's what you want. But I am thirty-two years old and I haven't done anything with my life. I've traveled the world but haven't really experienced it. I'm a lawyer but I work for my family business doing paperwork. I've never lived on my own or done things for myself. I've taken singing classes but never really sung to a real audience. I've done nothing in my life. There are things I want to do, and if I get married, I'll never get a chance to do them."

"Why not? Marriage isn't a prison."

"It comes with responsibility and a sense of obligation. Everything becomes about the family," she said bitterly.

And what's wrong with that? He had the freedom, money and time to do anything he wanted; it got lonely after a while. All his friends had long since married and he envied their complaints about soccer games, homework and birthday parties. They all had their own families and he didn't.

The jet nosed into the sky, and Ethan followed Divya's gaze outside the window as they left Las Vegas and headed into the clouds. Then she turned to him. "I've told you my poor-little-rich-girl story. What's yours?"

He smiled. "Well, this poor little successful billionaire started out with a wonderful family that didn't have much money but always had love." Bill had adopted him when he was ten. They'd moved to a new neighborhood and he'd started middle school without anyone knowing that Bill wasn't his real father. In all the interviews he gave—and answering Divya now—

his life story began at age ten. He didn't miss Wade. Once his mother had married Bill, Ethan had realized what a real father was supposed to be. But he'd always felt like the third wheel in his parents' marriage. And then his brother had been born.

"I have a younger brother who's married and has two awesome kids. They live down the street from my parents in Stillwater. It's a suburb of Minneapolis." He leaned forward. "I want what they have, but it seems no woman deems me worthy of lifelong commitment."

Divya raised her brows. "Oh come on! What is it women don't like? The fact that you're rich or that you're handsome?"

"You think I'm handsome?"

A smile played on her lips, and he itched to lean over and kiss her luscious mouth. "You're not my type, but most women would find you okay-looking."

"What is your type then? Tall and dark?"

"Maybe," she said coyly, and a fire licked in his belly at the way her mouth curved. "So what's wrong with you? Women think you're a spoilt rich kid?"

He shrugged. "I've only been rich for the last few years. Before my company took off, I was an average Joe with a nine-to-five job. Women loved dating me but said I wasn't the type of guy they'd marry."

Divya frowned. "Do you have strange habits or crazy fetishes?"

He shrugged. "Not that I know of. Although I do like a bit of adventure in bed."

She met his gaze. "Most women like a little fun in bed." Heat rose deep in his core and he had the insane urge to pull her by the loose T-shirt she was wearing and kiss her senseless.

She broke eye contact first. "I'll figure it out. I'm good at finding out what's wrong with men."

"Gee, thanks. There's nothing wrong with me. I think women don't know what they want."

"Or you only go out with women who are unavailable, so you don't have to commit."

The comment pulsed through him. "That's not true. I knew Pooja wanted to settle down and that's part of what attracted me to her. I asked her to move in after just three months of us being together because I was serious about her."

"Then, why did she marry someone else?"

"Because I took too long to propose."

"And why did you do that?"

Why indeed? "I needed a little more time. We'd only been living together for three months and had been dating for a total of six. That's not enough time to know that you want to spend the rest of your life with someone."

"Vivek knew in three weeks that he wanted to marry me. He didn't need more time."

"But you did."

"Because I don't want to get married. To anyone. If I were ready to commit, Vivek would've been just fine for me."

"You were in love with him then?"

"You have to be ready to fall in love. It's a mind-set, and I'm not into it. There is nothing wrong with Vivek. He's a decent person. He's kind and intelligent and met all of my criteria for what I'd want in a husband—*if* I were looking for one."

"So when you're ready, you'll be able to marry anyone who meets your criteria."

She leaned back in her seat and chewed on her lip, making him lose his train of thought.

"There's no straight answer to that. My criteria may change in the future. That's why I don't want to settle down right now. I don't feel like I know what I truly want."

You and most women I meet.

"I am ready for all of it, for love, marriage and children. I thought Pooja was too, but she kept our entire relationship a secret. We never went out in public together because she was afraid someone would post a picture on social media. She refused to introduce me to her family. I had good reason to doubt whether she was as invested in me as I was in her."

"She did that because she knew that you weren't going to propose to her. If her family is traditional, they would have exploded at her bringing home an American guy. She can't go through that kind of upheaval without a commitment from you."

It was almost exactly what Pooja had said to him. "What more could I do to convince her I was committed? I was going to stop her wedding and marry her today."

"No, you weren't."

How dare you! They'd known each other for a couple of hours, and here she was, challenging him on what he was or was not going to do.

"You might have been willing to stop her wedding, but that's as far as you were going to go. If you'd really wanted to sweep her off her feet and marry her today, you would've proposed to her when you saw her and let her decide how much she really loves her husband. It takes thirty seconds to get an annulment in Vegas. But you were almost relieved that she was happy, like you were off the hook."

He narrowed his eyes. "I believe in marriage. My parents have been married for almost thirty years and they are so happy together. My brother has been married for nine. He was my best friend until he met his wife. She knows him better than I ever did. She can read his moods, anticipate his needs..." He trailed off. "My parents, and my brother and sister-in-law, are a unit. They're connected at this deep level, and that's what I want. I didn't propose to Pooja because she and I didn't have that instant understanding and connection, but then I realized that maybe that comes with time."

Or maybe it's something I can't have with a woman. Nearly all the women he'd ever had a serious relationship with had married other men. Perhaps they could intuit something in Ethan that he couldn't figure out for himself. Perhaps they smelled his desperation and didn't like its stench.

Divya leaned forward and placed a hand on his. Her touch was soft and warm, and when he looked into her dark brown eyes, a slow burn flamed its way through his body.

"Maybe you've never opened yourself up to a woman so she can really get to know you. We women can tell when men put up barriers, and we don't like being with men we don't know and understand."

He pulled his hand back from hers. "I'm an open book. I'm talking to you, aren't I?" His tone was harsher than he meant it to be. He smiled. "Maybe it's easier to talk to you because we don't know each other."

She smiled back at him. "I have a talent for getting people to talk. It's the lawyer in me. If I'd gone into criminal law, I would've gotten confessions like this." She clicked her fingers.

He smiled. Divya really did have a way about her that made him feel at ease.

"Look, I've known you for all of two minutes and I can tell you didn't really want to marry Pooja. You wanted to know if *she* was willing to marry *you*."

Her words made his stomach churn. *Divya was wrong.* He was no longer the little boy who wanted his mother's new husband to love him, or the teenager desperate to be cool enough to get noticed by the popular girl.

Kathy knocked on the door, then entered with a tray of hors d'oeuvres and their drinks. They both sat in silence, Divya staring out the window, sipping her wine, while he moved himself to the couch and opened his laptop. He had an excellent management team who handled the day-to-day operations of his company. He'd let them know that he was taking ten days off, but he knew they'd call him if something needed his attention. Checking in on things was a comforting ritual to make himself feel useful. He also issued some instructions to his assistant in the New York office.

He looked at Divya, and as if feeling his gaze, she turned her head to look at him and gave him a smile that tightened his chest. What was it about her? The last thing he needed was to get involved with another woman. This one had declared from the outset that she wasn't available, yet he couldn't help but be attracted to her. Why had he taken it upon himself to fly her to New York? He could've satisfied his save-the-day complex by giving her the jet and a credit card.

She plopped herself on the seat beside him. He moved over so their knees weren't touching.

"Look, I'm sorry if I was a shit to you. You've been really nice to me. I can't stop my mouth sometimes. My brothers always tell me that I'm entirely too blunt and I need to temper my remarks."

"When do you get to the part where you sincerely apologize?"

She gave him an affronted look. "That wasn't sincere?"

"That was you telling me that you wished you'd sugarcoated what you had to say."

A smile twitched at her lips. "See what I mean? I can't stop my mouth."

Oh boy. Try as he might, he wasn't annoyed at her. As painful as it might be, she was honest and it was refreshing. But she was sitting too close to him. That intoxicating smell of vanilla and cinnamon was teasing his sensibilities. Her eyes searched his, and he voiced the words that were rolling around in his head but he didn't want to admit, even to himself.

"I didn't propose to Pooja because I held our relationship to the same standards as my parents' and my brother's and it didn't measure up. Yesterday I realized that I can wait my whole life for something that may never happen or I can seize the little bit of happiness that's right in front of me. When we got to the wedding, it was clear that Pooja had found with Anil what I'd been seeking with her." He'd seen the glittering adoration in Pooja's eyes and the shining smile on her face. She'd never looked that happy with him.

Divya shifted on the sofa, so her body was angled toward him, her knees now touching his. "I have no right casting stones on you. I had plenty of opportunities to stall my wedding. I did not have to do it in quite so dramatic a fashion. I clearly have my demons too." Her voice was soft and contrite.

"What demons do you have, Divya?"

She shrugged. "You talked about seizing the little bit of happiness that you can. My whole life has been about letting go of the happiness I want, in order to hold on to the joy I have." She looked away from him, and the shine in her eyes tugged at his heart.

"Aside from singing at Café Underground, what do you want to do? What's on your bucket list?"

She shrugged. "I've never made a bucket list. What's the point in wanting something you know you can't have?"

Her words struck a chord in his heart.

"Well, for the next few days, consider me your mag-

ical genie. Make a wish and I'll try to make it happen."
He grinned. Divya was easy to talk to and maybe she
could be the distraction he needed.

She smiled. "You're serious?"

He nodded.

"I guess I could really use a friend right now. Especially one with a private jet." She held out her hand.

"And I could use a friend who gives it to me
straight." He smiled and took her hand in his. It was
meant to be a handshake, but he found himself holding
her hand loosely, his thumb moving across the back of
her hand, feeling its softness. Divya's mouth opened
and he stilled, summoning every ounce of willpower
he had not to lean over and kiss her. Why wasn't she
pulling away? Was it his imagination or was she leaning even closer? Their mouths were inches apart.

He knew he was being impulsive again but he
wanted to feel her soft lips on his, to know whether
the earlier kiss that had shot zingers through his body
had been real or if he'd been high on adrenaline and
imagined the whole thing. He leaned forward.

Four

A second before their lips touched, she moved back. *What am I doing?* She'd almost kissed Ethan. Again. Just a couple of hours ago, she'd been about to take seven sacred circles around the marriage fire with another man. Granted, Vivek wasn't a man she wanted to marry, but it was a little too soon to get involved with someone like Ethan. *Especially Ethan.* Divya wasn't the good Indian girl her parents believed her to be. Without their knowing, she'd dated off the approved list. But Ethan was far beyond the unsuitable category.

Ethan shifted on the sofa so there was more space between them. He turned back to his laptop. An awkward silence settled between them.

He was gora. Not even in her wildest dreams had she thought about dating someone who wasn't Indian.

Her entire identity revolved around her family and culture. What could she possibly have in common with an American? *What does it matter? I'm not marrying him.* For the first time in her life, she was free of her parents' watchful eyes. In this moment, she was attracted to him, so what was the harm? There was no chance she'd fall in love with him.

Kathy appeared, saving them from more awkwardness. She asked what they wanted for lunch. Divya suddenly realized she was starving; she hadn't eaten anything all day. Ethan ordered a burger and she asked for the same.

"You eat beef?" he said, looking surprised, once Kathy had left.

She smiled. "Busted."

"Pooja didn't eat beef. She said most Indians, especially Hindus, don't."

"That's true. My parents would die if they knew I'm eating beef. Is it wrong that I love hamburgers? It's rare to find them in India. McDonald's serves lamb and chicken burgers."

He laughed. "I don't see anything wrong with having your own belief system. I wish Pooja had been more independent. She was always too concerned with pleasing her parents."

Divya frowned. "What's wrong with that?"

He held up his hands. "I don't mean any offense. It's just that our whole relationship revolved around the fact her parents would never approve of me."

"Did you try with her parents?"

"She never gave me a chance."

Divya chewed her lip. This was exactly why she had never fantasized about dating a *gora.* "I can see where Pooja was coming from. In Indian families, everything revolves around the parents' expectations. That comes with its bad parts, like having to conform to traditions you may not agree with. But there's also a lot of good. I've always felt loved and secure in my home. I've never felt loneliness in my life. When we were all on lockdown, it was the best time of our lives. We enjoyed being together. We stayed up playing games and having deep conversations about the silliest topics. None of us got cabin fever. When the lockdown ended, we were all sad that it couldn't go on longer." As she said the words, dread spread through her chest. *What if they don't forgive me?* "It's not about pleasing the family, it's about respecting who they are. It's a small price for the love and happiness you get in return."

He held up his hands. "I value that too. I'm very close with my family, and they've always been there for me. But they won't be dictating who I marry."

"Won't they?"

He frowned at her. "I don't understand what you're getting at."

"Did your family want you to marry Pooja?"

He shrugged. "It had less to do with my family than hers. My parents will accept whoever I choose."

"Would you be happy marrying someone who wouldn't get along with your family?"

He frowned, then shrugged. "That's difficult to answer in the hypothetical."

Bullshit. But she let it be. You could push someone

only so hard into seeing what was right in front of them. Plus, she couldn't risk pissing him off.

She changed the topic. "Thank you for taking me to New York. I can only imagine how busy you must be." She gestured toward his laptop.

He shrugged. "Not as busy as I'd like. The business is on autopilot. I hired a great executive team, who in turn hired some great people, and as the business has grown, I've become more of a figurehead for important decisions. They do the day-to-day."

"Is it hard for you to give up control over something that you created?"

He gave her a wistful smile. "It should be but it's not. I like focusing on the big picture. Besides, work can only give you so much satisfaction." He sighed. "I'd canceled all my meetings and taken ten days off to get married and go on a honeymoon."

"Sorry about that."

"No, you're right. If I really wanted to marry Pooja I would've proposed to her when she first threatened to leave."

Ah, he can admit when he's wrong.

Kathy returned with their burgers and they dug in with gusto. They chatted about their favorite books, movies and places they'd been. Divya was surprised at how much they had in common: they hated reality TV and loved witty historical dramas and suspenseful thrillers. He didn't share her obsession with horror movies, but no guy was perfect.

They landed at the private aviation terminal at Teterboro Airport, right outside the city, in New Jersey.

Divya knew from traveling with her parents that the main New York City commercial airports were very congested, so private jets used the smaller airports.

A tall older woman dressed in a business suit greeted them as they exited the plane. Ethan introduced her as his executive assistant Roda. Roda handed Ethan two rollerboard suitcases, a small box and the keys to a Mercedes roadster.

When they were seated in the car, he handed Divya the small box. "That's for you."

She opened it to find the latest smartphone and a black American Express card in her name. "Thank you. I promise to pay you back for everything."

He waved his hand. "Please, don't worry about it. Like I said, the last thing I need is more money."

The catch in his voice reverberated through her. She knew well that money couldn't buy what anyone really wanted, but Ethan seemed to resent his fortune.

The early September air was cool but the temperature was warm. "Do you mind if we go top down?" he asked. She stared at him, open-mouthed, then he pointed toward the top of the car. "It's a convertible."

Yet another thing she'd never done in her life: ride in a convertible. "Seems like fun. Let's do it."

He grinned. "I'll warn you, it'll mess up your hair. Most women hate it."

She shrugged and twisted her hair into a messy bun. He pressed a button, and she looked up at the beautiful sky and took a deep breath. *This is what freedom feels like.*

"I have a condo in the city we can stay at," he said as he put the car in drive.

Um, no. Given what had almost happened on the plane, she didn't want to stay someplace on his terms.

"My brother is bound to check for us at any properties you own in the city. I can call in a favor." She made a call on the new phone Ethan had given her, then instructed him to drive to one of the most luxurious hotels in New York.

It took them nearly two hours to navigate city traffic, but Divya barely noticed. She took in the sights and sounds of the chaotic city and savored the feel of the warm sun and cool air over her skin. She had been to New York before, but today she could really taste the smog in the air and feel the rhythm of the cars, people and bicycles.

She sent a WhatsApp message to her contact at Café Underground and crossed her fingers that he still remembered her.

It was night by the time Ethan pulled into the hotel driveway and handed his keys to the valet. Divya strode up to the check-in counter and asked them to call Rajiv Mehra. The clerk eyed her but delivered the message.

They didn't have to wait long before an Indian man, impeccably dressed in a custom-tailored suit and French-cuffed shirt, appeared. He hugged Divya. "It is so good to see you. I called Gauri as soon as you contacted me. She insisted we have dinner tonight." Rajiv sounded genuinely pleased to see her. She caught the look of surprise in his eyes at her clothing. "And

I insist you buy what you need from the lobby shops and charge it to me."

Divya hugged him. "You are such a good friend. I owe you big time." She knew he'd be insulted if she offered to pay him back with money.

Her phone pinged and she looked down to see a message from Café Underground.

"I definitely want to see Gauri and catch up with you two, but could we get together tomorrow? There's something I must do tonight."

If Rajiv was annoyed, he was too gracious to show it. "Of course. How about lunch tomorrow?"

"That would be great. Thank you so much for putting us up and keeping it secret. You know how my parents can be."

"How can I forget? You're safe here." He looked over Divya's shoulder to Ethan. "Is this your friend?" He arched his brows and switched to Hindi. "Now I understand why I wasn't your type."

She smiled and shook her head. "It's not like that." She quickly explained everything that had happened at the wedding.

Ethan cleared his throat and Divya realized she'd been rude in carrying on in Hindi with Rajiv. She introduced the two men. "Rajiv owns the hotel."

Ethan was duly impressed and said so without letting on that his own net worth was exponentially bigger than Rajiv's. Divya liked that Ethan didn't feel the need to advertise his success. On the plane, he'd changed into faded jeans and a plain T-shirt. No one would guess that he'd just flown in on his own private jet.

Rajiv handed them over to a staff member and invited Ethan to lunch the next day. Then they were led to a suite of rooms that made Ethan whistle.

"I've stayed in some pretty fancy hotels, but this is something else." They entered a great room that included floor-to-ceiling windows with a bird's-eye view of the city. A baby grand piano sat in the center of the room. There were two different seating areas, a small dining table, a bar and a kitchen. There were two bedrooms, each with its own sumptuous bathroom. It was all done in a warm, modern style with boxy furniture, wood accents and white linens.

"Rajiv is some friend to put you up here."

Divya nodded distractedly as she responded to a message on her phone.

"Friend of your family?"

She nodded. "Yes, our parents are close. My brother helped him get started with this hotel."

"And yet he's doing you a favor."

"He owes me," she said, smiling. "I'll tell you about it later. Right now I need to go down to the shops and buy something to wear." She grinned. "The stage manager at Café Underground remembers me and said he'd put me on the list to sing tonight." Her heart raced with excitement.

Ethan grinned and pointed to one of the suitcases they'd brought. "There should be a variety of things in there you can use."

Her eyes widened.

"My New York assistant, Roda, did some shopping

while we were in the air. I guessed your size but hopefully they fit."

"That was very thoughtful of you. Thank you. I'll…"

He shook his head. "Please, don't say you'll pay me back. We've discussed this, haven't we?"

She sighed. "I know you have lots of money, but I still feel like I'm taking advantage of you. We just met today. Let me at least help you figure out your love life."

He raised his brows. "You think there's something to fix?"

You don't? She stopped herself from saying that out loud. "I'm a great matchmaker. I set up Rajiv and his wife and they've been happily married for three years now."

"He has a wife?"

She tried not a smile at the relief in his voice. Had he been jealous of Rajiv?

"I've set up nearly all of my friends and most of the men my parents chose for me."

His lips twitched. "Was Rajiv one of those men?"

She nodded sheepishly. "He was, until I introduced him to Gauri and he fell madly in love with her."

"If you're that good, why didn't you set up your fiancé?"

She laughed. "I don't have a lot of friends in the US. Had he been based in India, I would've found him a woman who'd make him stop thinking about me."

"I doubt a man could stop thinking about you." Ethan's voice was so low and throaty that her heart stopped. She looked away from his sparkling blue eyes before she lost her mind entirely and decided to add Ethan to her bucket list. "Let's get dressed and get to Café Underground."

They each chose a bedroom. Hers had a dark wood platform bed made up in white linens with low-standing side tables and a dresser. Her bathroom was bigger than the bedroom and included white-and-gray marble tile, a tall oval Japanese soaking tub and a glass-enclosed shower. She set the bag Ethan had given her on a luggage rack and surveyed the clothes. There was a deep maroon cocktail dress with a cowl neck that would do for tonight.

The assistant had even included makeup. Unfortunately, the colors were too light for her skin tone, so she just went with mascara and lip gloss. Her hands shook as she applied the mascara, and she had to wash her face and do it twice. She had dreamed of singing in a real club but hadn't really thought she'd get the chance to make her dream come true. What if she tried to sing and nothing came out? Was her voice hoarse? She practiced a few notes. Was the sound strange or was it the acoustics in the bathroom? She took a deep breath and focused on getting herself ready. Tonight might be the only chance she had. She wasn't going to waste time.

The shoes included with the dress were too large, but she stuffed some toilet paper in the toe caps. She didn't want to be late to Café Underground.

When she stepped into the shared common room,

Ethan was by the bar. He looked casual but stunning in dark jeans and a fashionably untucked black shirt.

He whistled appreciatively when he saw her. "You look amazing. You're going to knock it out of the park."

"I know the expression, but I doubt it applies to me. I'll be happy if I don't get booed off the stage. This place is for hard-core artists and music lovers. The audience is serious."

He walked over to her and gently grasped her shoulders. "You'll be great, Divya. Just live for yourself tonight."

She took a breath and mentally repeated his words to herself. *Tonight is mine alone.*

The club wasn't far from their hotel, so they took a pedicab. The seat was cozy and she tried not to focus on the feel of Ethan's thigh against hers or the warmth of his body next to hers. She had a song in mind that she wanted to sing, so she went over the words in her head. It was a favorite of hers and she'd been singing it since she was a girl.

The pedicab driver skirted traffic, and got them to Café Underground in just a few minutes.

"This is where you want to make your debut?"

They were looking at a dark door with the words Café Underground flickering in neon lights above. She nodded reverently. It was exactly as she'd imagined it.

He opened the door and she took a breath as she stepped inside. The club was packed. A stage at one end of the room was empty but held a complement of musical equipment and was lit up with a spotlight. A bar on the other end was standing room only. The center of the room was dark and held high-top tables with barstools. All of the tables were full, and people crowded in between seats. The smell of stale beer hung in the air.

Divya's pulse quickened. *I can't do this.* Her parents never let her go out without a chaperone, and she wasn't used to such crowds. She suddenly felt unsure of herself. How was she supposed to handle this?

Ethan elbowed his way to the bartender to ask how to sign up for open mic. Divya stood back. Ethan was taller and more easily able to lean over the bar to hear what the guy was saying. The bartender pointed to another man seated next to the stage. He was short and wiry, with thick black-rimmed glasses, a mesh shirt and leather pants that couldn't be tighter if they were painted on.

Ethan made his way to the leather-pants guy, with Divya trailing behind. The crowd crushed around her and she found it hard to breathe. Ethan found her hand and squeezed it. They made their way to the stage and the man with the leather pants looked up. "Hey, you my Bollywood girl?"

She smiled. "Rick?"

"That's me, baby." He stood, leaned over and touched his cheek to hers. "Damn. You're even better-looking in person than on video."

"You are an even bigger flirt in person than on Zoom."

He smiled widely. "I'm gonna try and get you on when I can. It's a busy night, but chill. I got you."

Ethan navigated them back to the bar. A band on-

stage introduced themselves, and the lead began strum-
ming an electric guitar. The noise level in the room
increased several decibels.

Getting a drink turned out to take almost an hour. It
seemed very few people left the club but more joined
throughout the night. Each performer got two songs,
and the performances ranged from bands singing their
own songs to a cappella versions of popular hits to
solo instrumental and vocal performances. Divya's
feet were killing her, and by the second hour, she could
barely stand.

"Your feet hurt?" Ethan asked.

She nodded. "I'll be fine."

He walked over to a table and she saw him hand-
ing over several bills. Ethan managed to get them two
seats at a table where four other people were already
seated. Divya knew money was no object for him, but
it was the gesture that struck her. He paid attention to
her, not just what she said but how she was feeling,
how she was doing. How did an intuitive guy like that
not have women lining up to be with him?

He tried to introduce them to their tablemates only
to get shushed as they listened to the next band. He
leaned over and whispered to Divya. "This crowd is
no joke."

She nodded. "Broadway and other industry agents
and scouts come here looking for talent."

A solo musician stood onstage and tuned his guitar. "Hurry it up!" someone heckled. The musician
looked to be no more than a boy of eighteen or nine-
teen. He fumbled with the chords and his voice came

out strangled. The crowd immediately began booing, and the kid hurried offstage.

Divya's heart hammered. The room was getting hot.

"Don't worry, you'll be great." Ethan squeezed her hand.

"You've never heard me sing. I thought I could do this, but I'm not sure…" The words died on her lips as he put a finger on her mouth. She had an insane urge to take that finger and suck on it.

But just as fast, he pulled it off her lips. "I've seen your determination. You've given up a lot to be here. You can do this."

Tears pricked her eyes. Her family always told her how well she sang. Her parents paid for the best vocal teachers because she asked them to. Yet, none of them had ever believed in her the way this stranger sitting next to her did. He was still holding on to her hand, and she let his strength comfort her and calm the nervous churn of her stomach.

They sat and listened to the other musicians and with each new artist, Divya's doubts grew. The crowd was merciless, exuberant with their applause and brutal with their heckling. At least five performers were run offstage before they even finished their sets. She knew to expect this. It's what made Café Underground *the* place to test one's mettle. But now that she was here, she wasn't sure she could really do it.

Rick signaled to them. Divya looked up at Ethan, and he gave her a reassuring smile. "Go knock them dead." She knew without a doubt no matter what happened, there would be one person in the audience cheering for her.

Her feet hurt and her legs wobbled as she made her way onto the stage. The easy part of doing a vocal performance was the quick stage turnaround. No instrument tuning or setup required. The hard part was the fact that there was nothing but her voice. As she stood at the microphone, the crowd grew restless. They weren't going to be polite to her, like her family and friends. This wasn't like it had been on Zoom, when people were just glad to hear some music and connect with other people. And where Rick had had the ability to mute the crowd.

It was late into the night and the alcohol had been flowing for hours. They weren't going to be easy to please. This would be the moment when she'd find out whether she had any real talent. She'd worked hard for years with the vocal lessons; her singing was the only thing that hadn't been handed to her, and this was the moment she'd find out whether it, whether *she*, was worth anything. She took a breath and found Ethan in the crowd. He gave her a thumbs-up, and she began singing.

Five

Ethan didn't know what to expect, but even without ever having heard Divya sing, he knew she'd be great. What did surprise him was her choice of songs. She started with Leonard Cohen's "Hallelujah." It apparently surprised the crowd too, because as she escalated her voice into the first chorus, a hush blanketed the room for the first time all night. She closed her eyes as she sang the verses, varying her pitch to the crescendo of the words. With no instrumental accompaniment, her voice sounded pure and clear. It filled Ethan's soul with joy and arrested the audience into silence.

At the end of the song, the entire club burst into applause. Ethan stood, clapping as hard as he could. She wasn't just good. She was Whitney Houston, Aretha

Franklin good, with a rich deep voice that was pitch-perfect. He'd never heard anything like it.

The deal had been for her to sing two songs. For the second song she chose "Country Road," and the crowd went wild. This time she didn't stand still. She picked up the microphone from the stand and walked the stage. The crowd joined in with her, thrilled with her nostalgic choice. The other vocalists had all chosen more popular, contemporary songs.

When she waved to leave the stage, the crowd stood and shouted "Encore!" That was also a first all night. They'd liked other performers but hadn't asked anyone to stay.

Rick shook his head, but at the grumbles of the crowd he relented. "One more, but that's it," he bellowed and they all cheered.

Divya onstage was magic, her entire face transformed into sheer joy. This time she went with something more pop culture, but once again, Britney Spears's "Baby One More Time" literally hit the crowd just the way they wanted it. One of the a cappella groups joined in from the crowd, giving her some background vocals. This time Divya didn't just walk the stage, she danced too. If the audience loved her before, they were now smitten. She walked off to a standing ovation and calls for her to come back. Ethan was waiting at the bottom of the stairs, having correctly guessed that she'd be accosted the moment she exited.

Her eyes were wild with excitement, but he could feel the crush of the crowd wanting a piece of her, so he put a protective arm around her as he led her outside through a side entrance that he'd noticed earlier.

"That was great. Oh my God! They actually liked me." They had exited into an alleyway that smelled of urine and something worse, but she didn't seem to notice. She was positively giddy.

"You are amazing, Divya. You don't just have talent, you have a gift."

She twirled. "They didn't boo me offstage." The night had gotten cooler, but she didn't seem to care about the goose bumps on her arms. Her face was aglow and it brightened his heart. "Can you believe I just did that?"

He smiled, watching her dance in the dirty alley, her laughter and happiness so infectious that when she grabbed his hand, he pulled her into his arms. She flung her arms around his neck and stood on her tiptoes to hug him tightly. His breath caught in his chest. She felt so right against him. Her exuberance reached in and sparked a long-dead fire inside him. She loosened her embrace but kept her arms around his neck. He looked down at her shining face and knew he wasn't going to stop himself this time. He needed to kiss her. He lowered his head.

"Ah there you are!"

Both of them startled at the booming voice. The club door from which they'd just exited banged closed.

A tall, heavyset man with a round face and white T-shirt approached them. Ethan was immediately on guard. The man held out his card. "Jason Brugge from East Side Records. I've been coming to this club for years, and you are the first vocalist who's gotten me to put down my drink. I want you to give me a call. I'll set up an audition, see what we can do."

Divya stood frozen, so Ethan took the card. He would have Roda look up the guy to make sure he was legitimate. Anyone could print up business cards.

"She'll call you," Ethan said, as Divya seemed incapable of words.

When the man was gone, she snatched the card and looked at Ethan wide-eyed. "People come to this club for years hoping to get a card like this."

"I'm sure they do. But they don't have your talent."

She rubbed the card between her hands. "I'm going to frame this."

He took the card from her and pocketed it. "Let's go back to the hotel. We'll open a bottle of champagne and celebrate."

The alley was getting darker and danker by the minute. Divya hadn't noticed, but Ethan didn't like the look of the shadowy figures that had begun to make their way toward them from one end of the alley. He grabbed Divya's hand and walked quickly in the other direction. His management team had repeatedly asked him to have a security detail. His face was well-known in the media, and they were worried that he was a target. He'd resisted the intrusion into his privacy. That, and he could only imagine how his parents would feel if he showed up with bodyguards. They already thought him too pretentious.

He saw a taxi almost as soon as they exited the alley.

Divya was still giddy when they got to the hotel.

Ethan ordered a bottle of champagne and a couple of burgers from room service. As they ate and drank, they talked about the club and the other artists and the smell of beer that still clung to them.

Ethan had never had a hard time conversing with beautiful women. He'd dated his share of them. But it was different with Divya. He didn't have to work at making conversation; it just flowed. And when there were lulls, they sat back in pleasant silence until one of them had more to say. It was easy and comfortable.

Divya walked over to the suite bar. "Oh good. They have Black Label." She poured herself a small amount. "You want some?"

He crinkled his nose. "Mind if we skip that?"

"You don't like whiskey?" she asked.

He shook his head. "I can't even stand the smell of it. Bad memories."

She poured the whiskey down the sink and came back and sat next to him. He caught her gaze and sighed.

"You know I won't be satisfied until you tell me, so spill it."

"I didn't tell you the whole story about my childhood on the plane." He let out a breath and told her about Wade. "I like to pretend that my life only started with my stepfather. I've tried to forget Wade but I still associate the smell of whiskey with him. On the day my mother walked out on him, I went to give him a hug and he pushed me away so he could take a swig from the whiskey bottle."

"Wade never came back into your life?"

Ethan shook his head. He'd never told anyone what he was about to tell Divya. "When my younger brother was born, I was barely eleven. In my juvenile heart, I thought I needed to let my mom be happy with her new husband. I felt like an outsider. So I saved up my allowance and took a bus to the old neighborhood and found my dad. He was still living in the apartment he shared with my mom. Same old drunk but with a new girlfriend." He hazarded a look at Divya, inwardly cringing at the thought of the sympathy in her eyes, but he didn't see any. She just looked at him steadily, hanging on to his every word.

"I asked if I could stay with him and he said he'd never wanted me." There was one more part to the bile his father had spewed that day, but he couldn't bring himself to say the words out loud. His throat was tight and the sip of beer he took just burned in his mouth. Why had he told Divya? He didn't want her pitying him.

"Well, I bet when he found out you're now a billionaire, he regrets it," Divya joked. It was the perfect thing to say.

"Yep, he tried contacting me through my company, and I got the satisfaction of telling him that Bill is my father. He even tried going to the media and they dismissed him as a drunk."

"Well, it's great that Bill wanted you."

Actually, he didn't. But that was something he wasn't ready to share.

"So, what's next?" he asked, eager to change the subject.

"Now I can die a happy woman," she sighed. They were sitting on the sofa in the shared living area between their two bedrooms. The lights of the city glittered in front of them. He sat one seat down from her.

"Seriously, Divya, you were amazing tonight. You need to pursue a music career."

She chewed on her lower lip and he tried to ignore the stirrings deep in his core. "I don't want to be a vocalist. I wanted to test out my singing voice, but what I enjoy most about music is creating new songs. Fusing the rhythms of classical Indian music with Western beats."

"Why didn't you sing one of your own songs tonight?"

"First, I didn't have my guitar, but also I don't think the Café Underground crowd would've appreciated my Indian music. What I really wanted to do was sing onstage to a real audience. Thank you for giving me that chance, Ethan. Now I can go back to India and remember this happy feeling."

His heart dropped into his stomach. "What do you mean, *go back to India*? Wasn't the whole point of this to see if you had any talent? You want to give it all up and go back to your previously scheduled life?"

"The idea was never to pursue this as a career. It was something on my bucket list, and I did it."

"So tomorrow, you go back to your family and marry Vivek?" He couldn't keep the bitterness from his voice. Why had he let himself hope that Divya would be any different?

"I am not marrying Vivek, no matter what. And I'm

not leaving tomorrow. I want to make sure a few days have passed so the wedding guests leave and my parents can't guilt me into continuing with the festivities. I'll lie low, do some touristy things, let the whole wedding fiasco die down, and then I'll go beg forgiveness."

"Why won't you pursue your dreams?"

"There's a difference between a career and a hobby. My music is a hobby. It can't be my life."

"Why not?"

"Because it's not the kind of existence I want. Being on the road all the time, away from my family."

How could he argue with that? It's exactly what he didn't want, either.

She leaned down and rubbed her foot. He patted the seat next to him. "Hand me that foot."

She raised her brow. "You give foot massages too?"

"I know you probably grew up with your own personal masseuse, but I'll have to do for now." He gestured again to her foot, and she swung her legs onto the sofa, adjusting her dress as she did.

"You're one to talk. I'm surprised you don't have your own personal masseuse on the plane."

He took one foot in his hand and began massaging her heel. "I didn't grow up with money. My dad is a high school teacher and my mom works at a diner. While we always had food on the table, money was tight for luxuries. I worked jobs all through high school and college to help pay for things."

He tried not to think about how delicate her foot felt in his hand or how much he wanted to run his hand up her shapely leg.

"You must be thrilled that you can give your parents a better life now that you've done well."

His heart fisted. "I wish. They won't take money or anything from me."

"Why?"

"I don't know. It's not like its blood money. I earned every bit of it. They went through some hard times when my mom's diner had to close, and that was right around the time my company really started to take off. I know I got lucky at a time when other people were suffering…"

"Wait a minute. You shouldn't feel guilty about your money. You invented a product that's useful to people."

He hadn't said he felt guilty about his money, so how did she know?

As if reading his mind, she said, "I've been around wealthy people all my life. Until today, the only time I've seen someone carry hundred-dollar bills in their pocket and go around giving outrageous tips is in the movies. It's like you're trying to give your money away."

He smiled. He donated a big portion of his wealth to charity, had even started a foundation of his own that gave scholarships to underprivileged children. And yet his mother still worked at a diner. She was sixty-four years old, his father was close to seventy, and they were still working.

"I never expected my company to become an overnight success, especially during the COVID-19 crisis. I don't need this kind of money and never wanted it.

My parents taught me to work hard for my successes. I feel like I haven't done that. I just got lucky."

She shook her head. "Would you say that to me if I became a famous singer and made billions?"

He stared at her. "It's really hard to make billions from singing. Millions, maybe."

She gave him a patient smile. "You'd say I have talent and am making money from it. The same applies to you. Whatever's going on with your parents doesn't diminish your accomplishment."

He wanted to take her words to heart, but somehow he knew that if he was laboring away at a nine-to-five job, or perhaps if his brother, Matt, was the one giving it, his father would be more inclined to take his money. The thought burned a hole in his heart.

He switched his attention to her other foot, and she winced. He looked down to see that she had a scrape along the side of her foot. "Those heels were the wrong size, weren't they?"

She scrunched her nose. "A little bit. But it doesn't help that I've been wearing heels all day."

"Stay here."

He returned with a wet washcloth and cleaned and bandaged her foot.

"First thing tomorrow, I'm going shopping for some sneakers and maybe some yoga pants."

He laughed. "So you're not the kind of girl who wears couture around the house?"

"I'm not the type of girl who wears couture outside the house. Much to my mother's disappointment, I am a T-shirt-and-jeans type of girl."

Exactly the type he liked. She pulled her feet back and slid closer to him. "Thank you for today. Singing in front of a real audience, that's been a dream of mine. It's the only thing I've ever really wanted to do and you made it happen."

He shook his head. "You made it happen. With your voice, with your talent."

She leaned closer to him.

"Is it okay if I kiss you?"

Had she really asked him that? "What guy in his right mind would say no to a question like that from a beautiful woman?"

She gave him a slow smile. "You think I'm beautiful?"

I think you're freaking gorgeous.

He wasn't going to let this moment go. He leaned forward and their lips crashed together.

Divya didn't consider herself a sex goddess, but she was confident with her romantic experiences. Then came the kiss with Ethan.

She'd leaned into the kiss, fully intending to take charge. Except it wasn't the usual tangle of tongues and lips. Ethan took his time tantalizing her lips, sucking on them gently, flicking his tongue and letting her breathe in the heady scent of his aftershave. Her core tingled with anticipation. She pushed her fingers into his hair, eager to deepen the kiss, to bring his mouth closer. She heard him groan, and hot desire flared deep inside her. She wanted him. Bad.

He broke the kiss. "This probably isn't a good idea."

That was not the reaction she'd been expecting. He leaned back. "It's been quite a night," he said gently.

What am I doing? Maybe it was the high from Café Underground that had made her throw all sense of propriety to the wind. Here was a nice man who had helped her out and she'd put him in an awkward position by asking to kiss him. How was he supposed to respond to that? "Sorry, I shouldn't have kissed you," she said.

"I thought I kissed you," he said, moving back on the couch so no part of their bodies was touching.

"Why did you kiss me if you thought it was a bad idea?"

"I…" He ran his fingers through his hair. "I…we both almost married other people today. It seems like a bad idea to jump into something new."

It was as if someone had stuck a pin in her balloon. But she shouldn't be surprised. Ethan was wealthy and good-looking and dated women who looked like Pooja. How could she possibly compare? Her dating history consisted of Indian men who were into her because she came from a highly desirable family. Ethan was the first man who focused on her and not what her family had to offer. Of course he was rejecting her.

"Well then, I guess we both better get to bed, the sun will be up soon."

He nodded. "Good night, Divya."

She stared at him for a beat. He looked down at his phone. Guess there was nothing left to say.

"Good night, Ethan."

Six

She spent a restless night, despite the silky sheets and firm bed. She woke up hot and frustrated and dreaming of the kiss with Ethan. She could've sworn he was attracted to her. They'd had that moment on the plane and then again in the alley, before they were interrupted. Why was he pretending like they weren't hot for each other?

She took a long shower, slipped on jeans and a T-shirt, grabbed a light jacket and put on her heels from the wedding outfit. They hurt like hell but at least they fit. She mapped out the nearest athletic-shoe store. She peeked out of her room to see Ethan sitting at the bar. A room service cart sat in the middle of the room. *So much for avoiding him.*

"Good morning," she said breezily. He was dressed

in jeans and a baby blue polo that made his eyes look like the color of a cloudless sky. Her heart thumped loudly, but she ignored it.

He gave her a big smile and his eyes raked over her. Her stomach flipped.

"Good morning. I didn't know when you'd be up, so I ordered you a bowl of fruit."

She looked at the fruit and scrunched her nose. "Is there anything real to eat?" She picked up the phone and ordered eggs, pancakes and bacon on the side.

Ethan raised his brows. She gave him a challenging look. "Do you have a comment on my order?"

He shook his head and held up his hands. "I'm impressed. I don't think I've met a woman who likes to eat a real breakfast." He held out a piece of bacon from his own plate and she took the peace offering. She poured out a cup of coffee for herself. Yet another thing she loved abroad—coffee. She liked her masala chai and the instant whipped coffee in India, but there was something intoxicating about the smell of good brewed coffee.

"You've been hanging out with the wrong women."

"I certainly have," he muttered so quietly under his breath that Divya wondered if she'd heard it or imagined him saying it.

"So what's the plan for today?"

"I'm going shopping, and then I have lunch with Rajiv and Gauri."

"Am I no longer invited to lunch?"

No, you are not. I plan to ask Rajiv to help me lay

low for a few days and then go home. It's time for us to say goodbye.

"You can come if you want to," she said indifferently.

"I'll plan on it. While you're out shopping, you might want to pick up something for tonight."

"What's tonight?" she asked, unable to keep the curious interest out of her voice.

"I'd like to take you out to dinner."

He wanted to come to lunch with her friends and then take her to dinner? What was he doing?

"There's one more thing." He pointed to the couch.

"What?" Her hand flew to her mouth to keep from screaming. On the couch was a Martin guitar case. Her mouth hanging open in shock, she stepped to it and unbuckled the latches. Lying inside was a handmade acoustic guitar with a maple-gloss top and rosewood back and sides. She picked it up reverently.

"This is the top-of-the-line Martin guitar. How did you even know that I play acoustic?"

"Someone showed me this trick where you look up someone on social media and then search their friends' pictures to find out information that might not be on their own pages."

"How did you get this here so quickly?"

He shrugged. "This is New York. Not a lot you can't buy here in short order."

Especially when money is no object. She ran her hands over the wood. Her guitar at home was a Martin, but she didn't have the latest model. She picked a few strings, then began tuning it with expert hands. It was only when room service showed up at the door that she realized she'd been lost in the guitar. She hadn't even thanked Ethan.

After the waiter had taken the old cart and left a new one, she stood and went to Ethan. "I love the guitar, but I can't accept it. You've already done much too much for me, and you don't even know me."

He shrugged. "Money…"

"I know, money doesn't mean much to you but it's also the time you've taken to be with me, to fly me across the country, to search for the perfect guitar for me…" Her voice cracked.

How dare he do the most perfect thing in the world for her?

"Did I do something wrong?" he asked and she felt a tear slide down her cheek.

She shook her head, unable to speak through the big lump that had lodged in her throat.

"What is it?" He reached over and brushed the tear from her cheek, his touch so light and gentle that her chest squeezed even tighter.

"It's…" She struggled to find the word in English. *Aaapnapan* was the word in Hindi. Someone who treated you like their own, someone who knew you better than you knew yourself. He seemed to understand what she needed at a level that even her family didn't.

"Would you like to hear one of my songs?"

He grinned. "I'd like nothing more."

She strummed a few strings to test out the guitar, then sang one of the love songs she'd written. Her eyes closed, and the words bubbled up from deep in her plexus. It was a song she'd written for her brother Sameer when he was in a bad place. It had helped heal him and her. Ethan wouldn't know the words in Hindi, but they were what she needed to hear.

My heart doesn't know what to feel, my lips don't know what to say, but I'll be okay. I know I'll be okay because you're with me. I don't know what I want, I haven't for a while, but as long as I have you, I have hope of better things to come.

When she was done, there were fresh tears on her cheeks. It was as if something had burst open inside her. *Promise me, Divya, that if we get through this, we'll stop living for our parents and start living for ourselves.* She had forgotten that hospital-bed promise she and Sameer had made to each other.

"Wow, that was incredible."

She opened her eyes to see Ethan staring at her. "You're just being polite, you didn't even know what the words meant."

"No, but I could feel the pain in your melody, the hope in your voice." He paused. "What was the song about?"

She put the guitar in the case. "A couple of years ago my brother Sameer was in a bad accident. His whole body was broken. We weren't sure if he'd survive. I wrote this song for him. It is about hope and about not letting your fears stop you." She closed the guitar case and turned to him. "I think I'm going to give that record company guy from Café Underground a call. I'll ask Rajiv if he can put up with me for a few weeks so I can give this music thing a shot."

"I already asked Roda to check out that guy, plus I've put feelers out among my friends. Somebody will know an industry contact. And my jet is at your disposal. Whatever you need."

"We hardly know each other. Why are you doing all this for me?"

He shrugged, then he looked out the window like he couldn't quite meet her eyes. "Maybe it's because you're the first person I've met for whom I seem to be able to do something right."

There was so much longing in his voice that she wanted to hug him and tell him all the ways in which he was a great guy. But something held her back. He hadn't wanted her to kiss him. Maybe friendship was all he wanted to offer, and she didn't want to mess that up.

She poured him a cup of coffee from the room service cart and handed it to him. "Thank you. For everything. Now, let's eat this cold breakfast."

The rest of the morning went by in a blur as she shopped for some basic items. When she returned, she donned a cream silk shirt with dark blue–patterned pants. She let her hair loose and swiped some makeup on her face. Ethan had changed into dress pants and a collared shirt. He whistled when he saw her, and she couldn't help but smile. She'd put a little extra effort into her appearance.

They met Rajiv and Gauri in the hotel lobby.

"Divya, oh my God!" Gauri was petite, about five

feet tall with large luminous eyes. Her dark hair was pulled into a ponytail. She wore a black dress and dangling diamond earrings. Divya hugged her back. Rajiv had a town car waiting, which took them a few blocks down the road to one of the most exclusive French restaurants in the city.

At first they stuck to safe topics like politics, religion and money. But inevitably, her runaway status came up during a dessert of Grand Marnier soufflé and pistachio crème brûlée.

"So what mysterious plans did you have last night?" Gauri asked, throwing a suggestive look at Ethan. He nearly choked on his espresso.

"I was tired and went to bed early. Ethan had some business to take care of." She could feel Ethan looking at her, but he kept quiet.

Gauri narrowed her eyes at Divya but didn't say more.

"So, what's the plan exactly?" Rajiv asked. "Your parents and Arjun have been calling everyone you know."

Divya shifted in her seat. "I just want some time for my family to cool off, then I'll go home. I emailed Arjun to tell him that I'm safe."

"Yes, thank you, you used the hotel business center, and he tracked the IP address to New York and grilled me. You know I owe your brother a lot. I feel very bad lying to him."

Divya felt a pang of guilt. "I'm so sorry to put you in this position. We'll leave."

"You can stay as long as you need," Rajiv said halfheartedly. "I'm only saying there may be a better way of handling things."

Rajiv and Gauri looked at each other, then Gauri spoke up. "Look, Divya, I know we've been out of touch, but we were good friends once, so I feel I should be honest with you."

Ethan stiffened next to her.

"If you two are together, that's fine. We can accept that. Rajiv's brother married an American, and our family dealt with it. But this hiding is not good. It'll be hard for your family to accept Ethan if you continue on this way. He already has a reputation, and well..." Gauri trailed off as Divya shot her a murderous look.

Ethan didn't deserve to be attacked for her decisions. "Ethan and I aren't together. He accidently crashed the wrong wedding and I used the opportunity to run away. All he's been doing is helping me hide."

Gauri raised her brows. "Then, what are you still doing together? He's done his job. You are safe with us. Why is he staying with you?"

"I'm right here, you know," Ethan said quietly, but the anger in his voice was clear. "What Divya and I do is our business. We appreciate your hospitality, but we've clearly outstayed our welcome."

Divya winced. Ethan didn't know her friends and didn't understand that they were just looking out for her. His tone had been unnecessarily harsh.

Gauri reached out her hand and grabbed Divya's, clutching it as she turned toward Ethan. "Please, don't take it the wrong way. We are only concerned about our friend. It's in our nature to speak plainly. We didn't mean to offend."

"I know you didn't, and your point is well-taken. I will think about it," Divya said soothingly. She held up her spoon, eager to ease the tension around the table. "This crème brûlée is to die for."

After they were finished with lunch, Gauri cornered Divya when they returned to the hotel. Ethan looked at Divya, and she nodded to him, so he excused himself and went to the room.

"Divya, you know the rumors going around about you and Ethan."

She nodded. She had resisted the urge to google their names, but she could only imagine the media storm that was raging.

"What are you doing with him? If this continues, you will never get a good *rishta,* and your reputation will be ruined forever. It's not like you to be running around with a strange man. Especially not a *gora.*"

Divya took a deep breath. Every Indian parent with a daughter of marriageable age was on the hunt for a good *rishta,* a suitable match for their child.

"I don't want or need a good *rishta.* And Ethan is a perfect gentleman. I know what I'm doing."

"Do you? There might not be anything going on between you now, but I see the way he looks at you. It's only a matter of time before he makes a move, and then what'll you do?"

Jump his bones. The thought of Ethan making a move on her made her warm all over.

"I can take care of myself," she said cagily.

"Listen, Divya, I know it feels good to be out and about by yourself. To not have rules or restrictions. But trust me, Ethan is not the right man for you. He's hot, no doubt, but he's not marriage material."

"Why not? Because he's American?"

"Yes, that's exactly why. Rajiv's brother is married to an American woman, and let me tell you, it's like lunch was today."

"What was wrong with lunch today?"

"We had a polite conversation. We didn't talk about anything real. I didn't get to tell you that Rajiv's parents are really upset with my sister-in-law because she traded in the family jewelry they gave her for their wedding for something more modern. We didn't get to talk about how your parents are going to react when you go back. That's how it is in my house. We talk to his brother and sister-in-law about meaningless things, like they're strangers. There is always an awkwardness when you don't marry someone from your culture. And look, when I did try to talk about something real, he got angry."

"You were a little rude."

"I was being honest. But that's how it is. If he had been Indian, he wouldn't have taken offense like that, he would have understood where we were coming from."

Divya sighed. Why was she even having this conversation with Gauri? It's not as though she and Ethan were together or that she was even thinking about him in any serious capacity. Yet she felt an anger inside her and wanted to defend the idea that they could have something real.

Gauri touched her arm. "I'm just saying think about things carefully. Your parents will forgive you. Vivek still wants to marry you. The story came out that Ethan was dating some other Indian girl, so they know you didn't really run away with him. They all know it was cold feet and will forgive you. Take it from me. I couldn't wait to get away from my parents. Now I miss them every day. We only get to go to India once or twice a year and I savor every visit with them. You don't know what you're missing until you don't have it anymore."

Divya murmured a platitude, gave her friend a hug and said goodbye. Gauri hadn't said anything that Divya hadn't thought herself, but now every fiber of her being wanted to disagree with her friend, to prove her wrong.

When she returned to the room, Ethan was sitting on the couch with his feet up and his laptop open. She went and sat in a chair across from him. She owed him an explanation. To his credit, he didn't ask.

"I didn't want to tell them about the singing."

"It's something that's yours. You don't have to share it until you're ready."

And just like that, he struck a chord in her heart and she wanted to run back down and tell Gauri that this American, the one who didn't know her culture or speak her language and had known her for all of two minutes, understood her better than anybody else.

"Gauri didn't mean to offend you. She was just being blunt." Divya kept her voice light.

"She wasn't blunt enough. What she meant to tell you is that you're ruining your life by running around with me."

"You were a little forceful too."

"How did you expect me to react?"

"With some patience. If my brother finds out that Rajiv lied to him, it'll jeopardize their lifelong friendship. He's stuck his neck out for me. You could have been a little more polite."

"So it's okay for them to be rude to me?"

"They weren't being rude. They were asking a genuine question."

"Which was what exactly?"

"Why you're still here. You aren't romantically interested in me, and yet you're buying me guitars and making wishes come true. Why?"

He looked away from her, but she wasn't going to let him off the hook. She stepped to him, bent down and kissed him hard on the lips. He opened his mouth and kissed her back with the same hot intensity. This time, she broke the kiss.

"You're lying to me and yourself if you still think there isn't something between us," she said, then walked into the bedroom and closed the door.

Seven

Divya dressed for dinner in an off-the-shoulder black dress she had bought that morning and comfortable flats. It wasn't the look for a fashionista, but with her hair curled in stylish waves and her eyes rimmed with dark eyeliner, she knew she looked good. As she stepped into the common area of their shared hotel room, Ethan gazed at her with darkened eyes. "How many looks do you have, woman?"

Divya had avoided him for the rest of the afternoon. She'd heard him moving around but had kept her bedroom door firmly shut, spending the time tuning her new guitar and practicing her songs. She'd made her move, now it was his turn.

He offered his arm and she took it, noticing the clean scent of his soap and aftershave. She resisted the urge to lean into him so she could breathe him in. They took a pedicab, and she was somewhat surprised when they pulled up to a food stand outside Madison Square Garden. The city was alive with the sounds of honking cars and people bustling everywhere. The air was thick with the smell of exhaust fumes and cooking food.

"This is our big dinner out?" she quipped, tucking her hand into his arm.

"This place has the best hot dogs ever. And then I have a surprise for you."

They ate the hot dogs, standing on the sidewalk, watching the crowds flow out of Penn Station and stream into Madison Square Garden. There was a show on tonight and the headliner was a popular hip-hop artist.

"Have you ever been to a show here?"

Divya shook her head. Ethan pulled two tickets from his jeans and Divya's eyes widened. They made their way into the arena. Ethan's tickets were on the floor, toward the middle. When the opening act was introduced, Divya realized why Ethan had brought her here.

"Tina Roy. She's an Indian artist who mixes Indian and Western music," Ethan whispered to Divya.

The music was fantastic, and the crowd ate it up. Divya watched Tina dance around onstage, wearing a short fringed skirt and a tube top. She pictured her parents sitting in the audience, watching this woman grind with the male backup dancers and thrust her hips to the beat of the music. Her family wouldn't be proud; they'd be embarrassed. Her mother didn't even like Divya wearing skirts around the house. *Appearances are important, Divya. What will the staff think of you parading around with bare legs?*

Her mother would have a coronary if Divya ever wore an outfit like Tina Roy's, let alone performed onstage in it. Her cheeks reddened at the thought of her dad seeing her in such skimpy clothes.

Tina started her second number. The music, the clothes, the special effects were all designed to rile people up and Divya could feel the crowd practically vibrating. She closed her eyes and pictured herself on the stage at Café Underground, the energy that had pulsed through her as the audience appreciated her singing. She'd never felt that kind of power surge through her body. A crowd like the one at Madison Square Garden right now would be addictive.

Tina Roy's performance was amazing, but she wasn't a fan of the main act when he came onstage. "Do you mind if we leave?"

Ethan smirked. "This guy is no Tina Roy. Let's get out of here."

Ethan asked the taxi driver to take them back to the hotel. Divya laid her head back on the seat. Her heart raced. *Life is too short not to live it on your terms.* After Sameer had gotten out of the hospital, she'd spent all her free time working on her music. But as time went on, she'd slipped back into her mother's society life and the family business.

She looked out the window. "Can you pull up to the curb?" she asked the taxi driver. They were at Fifth Avenue and East Seventy-Second Street. Central Park stretched out on the right-hand side of the cab. "Can we go for a walk?"

Ethan paid the driver and exited behind her. They walked in silence, her hand tucked into his arm. Even at that time of night, the city was bustling. Birds chirped in trees, joggers pounded the trail, dogs walked with their owners, occasionally stopping to sniff something interesting.

"When I was growing up, my dad fulfilled my every wish. At the age of eight, I wanted a horse. I'd just read about Jhansi ki Rani, who's like the Indian equivalent of Joan of Arc, and I thought I would be great at horseback riding because I could feel the spirit of Jhansi ki Rani. My mother, who is always the realist in the house, told my father that it was a fad and not to go overboard. But of course, he didn't listen to her. He bought me a magnificent horse and hired a professional trainer to teach me how to ride. He even began renovating the ancient stables on our property. At first, I loved riding, but then as the lessons wore on, it wasn't fun anymore. It became a matter of working hard to learn how to ride. Each lesson left me sore and aching."

They walked toward the lake, which shimmered darkly against the soft lights of the street lamps on the trail. Her hand remained tucked in the crook of his arm.

"I continued with the lessons for years because I wanted to prove to my mother that I could do it. I never became a good rider. When my horse was too old to ride and retired, I was so happy. My father offered to buy me a new horse, and my mother simply turned to me and said, 'Tell him.'"

They walked alongside the lake. The night was rapidly cooling. Ethan put his arm around her shoulders, pulling her close. She didn't resist, grateful for the warmth and the feel of his solid body against hers.

"My mom knew all along that I hated riding, but she didn't say a word for ten years." She stopped walking and turned to stare at the lake. There was just enough light to see the reflection of the trees. Ethan remained quiet beside her.

"It's a lesson I'll never forget. There's a word in Hindi, *ghamand*. It doesn't have an English equivalent. It means pride, arrogance, vanity. It's being so stubborn that you cut your nose to spite your face."

Ethan turned to face her, and her heart raced. He kept a hand on her arm and stood so close that all she had to do was stand on tiptoe and she could kiss him. His hand moved up and down her arm and she felt the goose bumps, but her body was far from cold.

"Divya, I can't even begin to tell you how many times people discouraged me from moving forward with Deal Catcher. Amazon already existed and the market was flooded with apps. You have to believe in yourself. You can easily be Tina Roy one day."

She put a finger on his lips and felt him suck in a breath. Then she brushed her finger across his lips before retracting her hand.

"I'm not giving up on my singing. I loved being on-stage. But that's precisely why I don't want to ruin it for me. I don't want to be like Tina Roy. I remember listening to some of her early works and they were nothing like what she performed today. I don't want to write songs that appeal onstage and end up hating music."

"It doesn't have to be that way—"

"Ethan! I have a law degree, a career, a family. I have a lot going for me. Music will remain my hobby, something I enjoy."

"But you're so talented you can do anything you want."

Was it her imagination or had he stepped closer to her? She could almost feel the rise and fall of his chest. She put her arms around him and he closed the distance between their lips.

This time, he didn't hold back when he kissed her. He pulled her close and she gave as good as she got. Their lips were in perfect harmony as they explored and tasted each other. She pressed her body to his and fire licked deep in her core. She molded herself to him, and felt his attraction, hard against her belly.

He stepped back from her, his breath heavy.

"There is one thing I really want to do that I'm not sure I can."

His lips twitched. "What's that?"

"I want to seduce you."

Eight

Do not kiss her again. Ethan wanted to tell the inner voice ringing alarm bells in his head to shut up. She lifted her chin, her eyes challenging him to take another taste of her wet lips. He could handle an affair with her, couldn't he? He knew where she stood on the topic of marriage; there'd be no expectations between them, just a physical relationship. He looked into her eyes and his heart jolted.

"It's getting late. Let's go back to the hotel."

She raised a brow but didn't say anything. They retraced their steps back to Fifth Avenue and caught a taxi back to the hotel. They were at the lobby elevators when one of the front desk clerks came rushing up to them. "Miss Singh!"

"Yes?"

"Mr. Mehra needs to speak to you urgently. He's on his way. Please wait right here."

Rajiv appeared a few minutes later, his suit still perfectly pressed, despite the late hour. "Divya! I didn't know how to reach you." He sounded frantic.

"What's happened?"

"The show you were at tonight, someone recognized Ethan." His gaze flicked to Ethan. "Arjun is tracking all mentions of Ethan on social media. He and Vivek are on a plane from Vegas."

"Vivek? Why is he coming?"

Rajiv shrugged. "Arjun didn't get into the details, but I think Vivek wants to talk to you. Maybe he feels he can convince you to get married."

Divya sighed. Rajiv gave Ethan a pointed look, then lowered his voice, as if doing so would exclude Ethan from the conversation. "I think you should be honest with your brother. Running away is not the way to handle things."

Divya glanced at Ethan. He should nod, tell her Rajiv was right, because he was. She needed to confront her family, not hide from them. Yet he couldn't bring himself to do more than blink at her.

"I can't, Rajiv. I'm not ready to face my family yet."

Rajiv pressed his fingers to his lips. "Then, I need you not to be here when Arjun arrives."

Divya placed a hand on Rajiv's arm. "I'm so sorry. Of course we'll get out right away."

"I've arranged a limo for you. A friend of mine has a house in the Hamptons where you can hang out until you're ready to go home. I'll arrange whatever you need." Rajiv gave her a pointed look and it wasn't hard to understand the subtext of his words. Divya didn't need to rely on Ethan. There was no reason for him to hang around anymore.

Once again, Divya looked at Ethan. *It was probably best that they parted ways.* The more time he spent with her, the greater the chance that he would lose his heart to this girl who was very much unavailable.

"Thank you, Rajiv, but I don't want to involve you more than you already are. I know your friendship with my brother is important."

"Divya…"

Ethan took a step forward. "Don't worry, Rajiv. I'll take good care of her. I can have my jet ready to go in an hour."

Rajiv looked between Divya and Ethan, then spread his hands. "Good luck to you." Then he turned and said something to Divya in Hindi. Her eyes widened and Ethan could've sworn he saw her blush. She responded in Hindi, then hugged Rajiv. Without a glance at Ethan, she pressed the elevator button.

Ethan didn't ask what Rajiv had said and Divya didn't volunteer. They didn't have a lot of stuff, so it didn't take long to pack. Ethan made arrangements for the jet and called the valet to bring the Mercedes.

"Are you sure you want to keep running? I'd be happy to wait and take you wherever you want to go after you sort things out with your brother."

Divya began shaking her head before he even finished the sentence. "I'm not ready for this to end yet. I'm enjoying my freedom."

"Why does it have to be an all-or-nothing deal, Divya? Why can't you tell your brother that you're ready to be your own independent woman?"

"Because that's not how things are done in my family."

The valet brought the Mercedes, and he loaded the luggage and opened the door for her. The night was cold, so Ethan didn't drop the top on the convertible. As he eased out of the hotel driveway, he turned toward her. "What're you so afraid of?"

"I'm afraid of how much I love my family. Arjun has a way of convincing me that he'll work something out to get me what I want. But it's never exactly what I want."

"What do you mean?"

"After I finished law school, I wanted a job. I was even offered this great position with a law firm, but my parents didn't want me to take it. They didn't understand why I wanted to work, given that we have plenty of money. My mom wanted me to be a socialite like her so I could find a nice husband. Arjun brokered a deal with my parents where I could work, but for the family firm. Don't get me wrong, I appreciate it was a big battle for him to get me that concession, but the whole reason I wanted a job is to have some independence from the family."

"I still don't understand why you didn't just take the law firm position. It's not as if your family would've locked you at home."

She blew out a breath, but Ethan wasn't going to let her off the hook. Divya didn't seem like the type of woman who had been cloistered all her life. She was confident and self-assured enough to get what she wanted. *Including me.* There was something she wasn't telling him.

"No, of course not. We're not that type of family. It's more that they worry and care about me, and once I see my brother again, he'll remind me of all the reasons why I should come home." She looked out the passenger-side window, clearly hiding her face from him.

"What aren't you telling me?"

"It's complicated, and now's not the time. Let's discuss where we're going."

He wanted to know more, but clearly, she didn't trust him enough to share what was really going on.

"I have something you should add to your bucket list."

She grinned at him. "What do you have in mind?"

"Trust me?"

She leaned back in the car seat. "I'm all yours."

If only that was true.

Nine

It was past midnight when they arrived at Teterboro, but Roda was waiting there. She handed Ethan several shopping bags and took the keys of the Mercedes.

Kathy greeted them warmly when they got on the plane. They ordered coffee and dinner.

He took a seat in one of the reclining chairs that faced the back of the plane and Divya sat opposite him. They were quiet until Kathy returned with their food. "We're waiting for clearance from the tower. It might be a while before we're ready to take off. The pilot is expecting a bumpy ride because of a weather system coming in from the south. I'll be in the jump seat. Ring the call button if you need anything."

They dug into their food, both of them famished.

The hot dog at Madison Square Garden had been hours ago.

"You want to tell me where we're going?" Divya finally asked.

He smiled. "Let's just say we're going to go do something that'll help you face your fears."

"Please, don't tell me we'll be in a tank full of sharks."

He laughed. "Now, why didn't I think of that?"

She leaned over until her face was inches from him. Her breath smelled of coffee and her vanilla lip gloss, and all he could think about was pulling her onto his lap and kissing her until he didn't have any air left in his chest.

"You told me to trust you," she said.

He swallowed, trying to remember what they were talking about. "Don't worry. I'll be with you." He placed his hands on her shoulders and gently pushed her back into her seat. He couldn't have her so close to him.

"You want to tell me what's going on between us?"

"Excuse me?"

"You kiss me like you're going to swallow me whole, and then you pull away. What's going on?"

He sighed, not sure if he loved or hated Divya's straight talk.

"I'm attracted to you, Divya, but just a few days ago I broke up your wedding. What kind of man runs away with the wrong bride, then gets involved with her? I don't want to get into something messy and make you feel uncomfortable."

"How chivalrous of you. First of all, I decide what's comfortable for me, and second, why do you assume it'll be messy? I'm an adult and so are you. I enjoy sex. I hope you do too. Why can't we enjoy it together?"

Damn. When she put it that way, he had a hard time coming up with a coherent answer. How did he explain to her that he felt a connection to her? Perhaps it was real, or maybe it was his traditional pattern of falling for women who were unavailable. He knew their chemistry was real, and he was afraid to find out just how explosive it could be.

He stared at her, and the fire in her eyes ignited something deep and powerful in his core. For the first time in his life, he wanted to fight his impulses. A loud warning blared in his head, but he was having a hard time hearing it. Divya's glossy pink lips were calling out to him.

"Look, there are no expectations between us. I don't think you're taking advantage of me, we've clearly got chemistry. Why not enjoy ourselves for the short time we have together?"

Because I may not just want you for a short time.

Of all the men she'd been with, none got her as hot and bothered as Ethan. Maybe because for the first time in her life, she wasn't looking at someone through her family's eyes. He wasn't a man to be evaluated for marriage. He was a man she could just be with. No expectations, no boundaries. Total freedom.

It wasn't a question of attraction. She'd felt his attraction hard and clear when they kissed. *Does he think I'm too inexperienced to understand what sex means?*

She left her seat, leaned over and pressed her lips to his. His eyes darkened and she knew she had him.

"I'd like to add the mile-high club to my bucket list."

She gave him her most sultry smile, then turned her back to him, took her shirt off and let it drop to the floor. His eyes were glued to her, but he sat frozen in his seat. She took off her lacy bra and flung it at him, then crossed her arms over her chest. She stood for a second and looked over her shoulder at him. The sharp intake of his breath made her smile. She walked to the bedroom at the back of the plane.

As expected, he wasn't far behind. She'd barely stepped into the tiny bedroom when she felt his arms around her, his chest to her bare back. The bed took up most of the space in the room. There was a mirror opposite the door. She saw their reflection as his hands crisscrossed her waist. He kissed the spot where her neck met her shoulder, and a delicious quiver coursed through her body.

He met her eyes in the mirror. "You're a dangerous woman, Divya, but I'm no slouch in the seduction department." He ran his hands over her narrow waist and flat belly, then worked upward and cupped her breasts, running his thumbs over her sensitive, taut nipples. Her core melted and she moaned. She reached back and weaved her fingers into his hair, tugging at it to let him know he was driving her crazy as his lips worked their way up her neck to nibble on her ears.

She moved her hands down and found him hard and

ready. She caressed him through his jeans and smiled as he groaned. He loosened his arm and she turned around and tugged his shirt off. His chest and hard abs had a sexy smattering of hair that was just right. She ran her hands over him, noticing the darkness of her skin against his paleness. "Wow, you are really white."

He chuckled. "I'll work on my tan."

She ran her hands down his pecs, over his belly, following the trail of sandy-brown hair from his washboard abs to the top of his jeans. She popped the button, and he shook off his shoes while she tugged his jeans off.

"Hmm, I like a boxers man."

She touched his velvety hard-on, tentatively at first, but then she took it firmly in her hand.

"Divya!" He breathed her name in a begging moan. She moved her hand up and down until he placed his own hand on hers, stilling her. She looked at him questioningly, but he moved her hands to her own waistband. He undid the button on her jeans and she slid them down. She was wearing one of her new purchases, the red lace panties. His appreciative moan told her it had been a worthwhile purchase. He touched her core through the soft fabric and she melted. She was hot and swollen and wet and she wanted him hard and fast.

She hooked her fingers in the waistband of her panties to take them off, but he stopped her.

"Not so fast." He worked his fingers over the outside of her panties, circling her tight bud, pushing his finger slightly inside.

They felt the plane gain speed as it began to taxi down the runway.

Enough. If he was going to drive her mad, she was doing the same to him. The bed was behind him. As the plane rose in the air, she gave him a hard push and he stumbled backward. She pushed him again until he was sitting on the bed. She straddled him. Her panties were wet and she ground against him, enjoying his moan of pleasure. His mouth found her breast, and his tongue licked and teased while he cupped the other in his hand, his fingers rubbing her nipple until she felt intense pressure in her core.

It was tempting to give in to her release, but she knew it would be so much better with him inside her. When he came up for air, she got up, reached into her jeans for a condom and tore off the outside packaging. She'd been prepared for this moment. She took off her panties while he watched, his sky-blue eyes as dark as hers. Then she touched herself.

"Take off your boxers."

He complied immediately, then reached over and took the condom from her. He quickly sheathed himself, and she stepped back toward the bed, spread her legs on either side of his knees and straddled him as she took him inside her in one slick motion.

He filled her just right, and the feeling was so intense, so perfect that she clutched him with her muscles, dug her fingers into his shoulders. She rocked and shuddered and shattered violently against his arousal, her climax so powerful that she screamed. He vibrated inside her and that brought a new wave of heat and pleasure coursing through her.

She rested her head on his chest, too blown away to speak. He circled his arms around her as she slid off him, pulling her close. She wrapped her arms around his chest and inhaled the scent of his soap and sweat and felt her core twitch with desire.

The plane shook as they hit a rough patch of air. She moved involuntarily and felt him harden.

Whoa. She'd had sex before. She liked sex. But what she'd had before was the kind of run-of-the-mill orgasm that her vibrator could accomplish. Ethan... Ethan was the master of finding all the right spots.

As she slid off him, he caught her wrist and she looked at him. His eyes smoldered with the same emotions that raged through her: unsatiated desire, surprise at how good it was between them, fear because of how good it was between them and perhaps a little anger that she'd brought them to this point. She gave him a half smile. Who knew what the future held for her, but at the moment, she had all the freedom in the world. She wouldn't have to wonder what it would've felt like to be with Ethan. The longing would've consumed her. Now she could get it out of her system, just like she had with her dreams of being a singer.

He let go of her wrist, stood and went to the attached bathroom to get rid of the condom. Divya stood uncertainly, wondering whether she should get dressed. Should they sit and have a naked chat? What she really wanted was to go for round two. Make sure she hadn't imagined round one.

He returned from the bathroom, tossed himself onto the bed, got under the covers and patted the space beside him. She crawled into bed and he pulled her against him, her back to his chest. He curled himself around her and she felt him getting hard, which made her own core tighten with anticipation.

"You had to do that, didn't you," he whispered in her ear, sending hot shivers down her spine.

"Would you rather I hadn't?"

"It's hard to answer that now, when the reality was better than my fantasy."

"It's better than wondering what could've been," she said.

"Aren't you the one who advised me not to go for women who are unavailable?"

She had, hadn't she? And she definitely wasn't available. Had she been so selfish in her desire for him that she hadn't noticed him developing real feelings for her? She eased herself from his arms and sat up on the bed so she could look at him. "You're not falling for me, are you?"

"Don't you have a high opinion of yourself."

"Well, I am pretty lovable."

"And hot, don't forget hot." He reached for her and pulled her onto him so that their naked bodies molded together. She ground against him, getting him harder, then leaned toward him so her breasts tantalized his chest. He sucked on one hard nipple, then the other. She was already slick. He rolled her over so she was underneath him. From there, he went on an exploration of her body with his mouth that left her writhing with pleasure. He worked his way down from her breasts to her belly and finally to her core, where he teased her with his tongue and sucked her with his lips. When she couldn't take it anymore, he reached into the bedside table, pulled out a condom and put it on, then entered her slowly. She cried out and pushed her hips up to meet him, taking him deeper inside her.

He moaned and she increased the tempo. It didn't take long for both of them to shatter, the world exploding even more powerfully this time than it had before.

Divya gasped for breath as she finished. She lay there as Ethan took care of the condom, then returned. He slid into the bed and she turned to face him, tucking her leg between his. She wanted to stay with him for as long as possible and soak in the feeling of pure bliss. She placed a hand on his chest and traced the hair across his ribs. The men she had been with all had dark hair and dark brown nipples, like she did. Ethan's were pink and rosy and she ran her fingers over them. "There is such a difference in our skin color."

"Does that bother you?"

"It's just… I don't know."

"You know, our differences are only skin deep. We have more in common than you think." He took her hand and weaved his fingers through hers. "Family means everything to me, just like it does to you. And I know what it's like to want something so badly that it scares you to admit how much you need it."

Her heart slammed against her chest. Ethan stilled. She withdrew her hand from his and turned her back to him. "I think the day is catching up with me."

"I'm not going to let you go that easy, Divya." Ethan muttered. He put his arm around her and pulled her close.

His warmth felt so good, so comforting, that it wasn't long before she fell asleep dreaming of singing onstage like Tina Roy, with Ethan cheering her from the audience.

Ten

"Where are we exactly?" The first rays of sunlight were barely visible in the sky when they deplaned. They'd made a fueling stop somewhere, but Divya hardly remembered. She'd been so exhausted that the final descent had barely registered.

The air was hot and humid. An attendant waited with the keys to a Porsche Carrera, the convertible's top already down. Divya was wearing jeans, a long-sleeved blouse and a sweater and felt very overdressed for the weather.

She looked at Ethan, meeting his eyes for the first time since she'd slid out of bed. He walked to the passenger door of the car and held it open for her. "We're at a private airport in Key Largo. Let's get on the road. There's a sunrise view I don't want you to miss."

She lowered herself onto the hard leather seat and took off her sweater. "What about our luggage?" she asked as he slid into the driver's seat and started the engine.

"We'll be back on the plane by the evening. I have to be in Minnesota tonight. It's my parents' wedding anniversary."

"Oh," she said. Was she going with him? Did she even want to go with him? She studied his profile as he steered the car out of the private airport. He was objectively the most handsome man she'd ever been with. His jawline was sharp, his nose perfect, his lips utterly kissable. Warmth pooled deep in her belly as she thought about his mouth on her body and in between her legs. Her entire body still tingled from his touch. He was a considerate and giving lover and she knew without a doubt that she'd always compare any man she ever slept with from this point on to Ethan.

What if he's the last man I sleep with? She pushed the idea firmly to the back of her mind because it was too pleasant a thought. Had she made a mistake by seducing him? He'd been good to her. She didn't want to break his heart, but there was no way they could be together long-term. He was wrong about their differences being only skin deep. He knew her only as Divya the woman, not Divya the sister or daughter. Would he understand her commitment to her family? How would he deal with her parents? She'd seen how defensive he'd gotten with Rajiv and Gauri. Her mother didn't mince words and she didn't let anyone talk back to her. *Why am I even thinking this way?* It wasn't as if she was getting serious about Ethan. It was good sex. Okay, amazing sex. But that's all it was.

Ethan motored south onto US Route 1 just as the first rays of the sun began to brighten the sky. She gasped as she caught sight of the crystal clear water all around her. It seemed like the road was floating on top of the ocean.

"The Atlantic Ocean is to our left and the Gulf of Mexico to our right. This is called the Overseas Highway," Ethan said.

"Are we even on land?"

He smiled. "If you're impressed now, wait until we get on the Seven Mile Bridge in a few minutes. You'll feel like you're about to fall into the ocean."

As the sun burst into the sky, the scene in front of her transformed into hues of orange, red and purple. The water changed from a dark blue green to a lighter blue. There was little traffic on the road, so Ethan drove slowly. "This the most beautiful sunrise I've ever seen, I wanted to share it with the most spectacular woman I've ever met."

Her chest constricted at the thickness in his voice. She was glad she couldn't see his face and he couldn't see the tears that had suddenly sprung in her eyes. Plenty of men had told her how beautiful she was, but Ethan hadn't just meant her looks. She knew that in her heart, and that made his compliment sting. He was a good man. Had he been a *suitable boy* who her parents had set her up with, she would've been having a very different conversation with herself. But there was no scenario in which her family would accept a *gora.* Arjun had almost been disowned for wanting to marry an Indian girl who was divorced. Divya's sister-in-law, Rani, was an amazing person who spoke their language, understood their culture and traditions. Yet Rani struggled with truly fitting into the family. How could Ethan ever become a part of her world? Gauri's comments about the impersonal nature of their relationship with her white sister-in-law came to her. Ethan would always be an outsider standing next to her.

She saw the sign for the Seven Mile Bridge, and Divya leaned over as far as she could to look out the window. "Oh my God, I can almost see the fish, the water is so clear."

"We won't have time to go swimming today, but you should come back and really explore the Keys."

He'd said *you*, not *we*. Somehow, she knew she could never come back here without Ethan. This place, this feeling of pure bliss, would always remind her of him. She lifted her face to the sky and breathed in the warm, salty air. Her home in Rajasthan was a desert, so there was always a grittiness in the atmosphere. She'd been to Miami before with Arjun to check out a potential hotel he was looking to buy, but they'd never taken the time to travel to the Keys. "How did I not know that such a spectacular place existed?"

"You have to get out of your comfort zone to find this kind of paradise."

This was truly paradise. But it wasn't real life. It didn't include the people she loved. It was a momentary escape. She closed her eyes to savor the moment and lock it away in her mind so she wouldn't forget.

She took out her phone and snapped a picture of the sunrise, then reached out her arm and leaned close to Ethan for a selfie.

"Are you going to give our social media fans a honeymoon picture?" he said laughingly.

"I want to remember this moment forever."

"Why?"

What did he mean, *why*? "It's an amazing sunrise."

"Is that the only reason?"

Her stomach clenched. Why couldn't things just be easy, uncomplicated and temporary between them? "I enjoy being with you, Ethan. I love our time together and I want to remember it for when…" Her throat suddenly went dry.

"For when it ends, and you go back to your regularly scheduled life."

"It's not as if it'll be goodbye forever. We will keep in touch, stay friends."

He stayed silent, his lips set in a straight line, and her stomach flipped. He knew it could never be serious between them, *didn't he*? She'd been upfront with him that she was not the marrying type, and he wanted someone forever. He was done with jetting around and temporary relationships. She was done sitting at home and letting other people make decisions for her. Perhaps it had been a bad idea to sleep together. And yet as she looked at him, all she could think about was running her hands all over him.

Once they got off the Seven Mile Bridge, he took a right turn onto a gravel road. He pulled up to what looked like a log cabin. A hand-painted sign read Sky-dive Keys. She stared at it.

"You can't be serious. We're going skydiving?"

He nodded. "That beautiful view we just saw is even more spectacular from the air."

"Are you crazy? I don't know how to skydive."

"You're not going to do it alone. We're going to be strapped together in tandem."

You are nuts! There was no way she was going to do something like that. She wanted adventure, but this was extreme. What was Ethan thinking?

A man with long blond hair and a scraggly beard appeared from the cabin. "Ethan, my man."

Ethan exited the car and did some sort of secret handshake with the guy, who looked more like an overweight surfer dude than a lean mean skydiver.

"It's been a while. Plane's gassed and I got your gear laid out." Divya got out of the car and surfer dude turned to her. "Name's Buck."

He held out his fist and she gave him an awkward bump with her own. "You guys picked a nice day. Sky is clear, air is warm and you've got just enough wind to get a nice ride."

"Awesome!" Ethan said. "Let's go! Thanks for opening early. I want to get our run in before the tourists get here."

"I got you, man."

As Ethan began walking toward the cabin, Divya grabbed his arm. "Are you really serious about this?"

"Relax. I have a level D skydiving license. I've done about six hundred jumps. You're going to be strapped to me the whole time and I'll take care of the parachute pulling. All you do is enjoy the experience. It'll be like taking a roller-coaster ride."

All she had to do was strap herself to him and enjoy? That did sound good. Except they'd be falling out of the sky. Her mouth went completely dry.

As they turned a corner, she saw two long pieces of cloth on the ground attached to a backpack.

"Is that our parachute? Is that how it's supposed to be?"

He laughed. "I like to pack my own parachute and make sure it's done right. There's two main parachutes, one you'll be wearing and one that I'll be wearing. Plus we each have an emergency parachute that someone else inspects and packs. It's all perfectly safe. We only need one parachute and we'll have four between the two of us."

She looked around. There was an airstrip and a plane that looked like it had seen better days. Beyond the airstrip, the Gulf of Mexico shimmered as the sun rose higher. "Is this the only skydiving place around?" Divya asked.

He shook his head. "I know this place looks like a dump, but Buck and I went to high school together. He's a good guy and he knows what he's doing. I've been jumping here for years."

Ethan ran his hand down her arm. She turned to face him and he pulled her close. His body felt solid against her and a shiver rose deep from her core. She pressed herself to his body and stood on her toes to whisper into his ear, "You know, sex on the beach is also on my bucket list." She kissed his ear and felt his reaction push against her belly. He pressed his lips to hers, then disengaged.

"Nice try, but we're doing this."

Her eyes widened. "This is madness. I'm not into sports. I don't even play badminton."

He stepped closer and cupped her face. "At any point you want to abort, just say, 'bridesnatcher.' It'll be our safe word."

She couldn't help but laugh.

"You trust me?" he asked.

His eyes, the color of sky, sparkled like the shimmering water behind her. It was so easy to get lost in them, to forget all the alarm bells ringing in her mind. She nodded.

Things moved quickly after that. Buck returned with a tablet and made her watch a safety video while Ethan meticulously inspected, folded and packed the parachutes. The video showed her how the gear would work, how to position her body during the dive, how to open her chute and how to land. Buck then did some practice exercises with her.

"What happens if we free-fall too long and don't open the parachute in time?"

"If you open the chute too late, your descent will be too fast." Buck slapped his hands together. "You pancake if you land on the road or become shark food if you land in the water."

Her mouth fell open.

"Stop it, Buck," Ethan said. "I'll open the parachute in time. You don't have to worry about that."

Things were moving so quickly, Divya couldn't even process everything that was happening. She was exhilarated as much as she was scared. When else would she ever get to skydive? Her parents thought skiing was too dangerous a sport. She was free to do what she wanted.

They put on their harnesses and chutes, did a final safety check, then climbed into the plane. The interior of the plane was like the inside of a paper towel roll. There were no seats—it was even more basic than the outside. Ethan showed her how to scoot onto the metal floor and sit with her legs in front of her. They could see clear into the cockpit.

Ethan pulled Divya close to him, her back to his chest, his legs beside hers.

"All right, sit tight, flight time is ten minutes." Buck looked back from the cockpit, and Divya closed her eyes.

As the plane taxied and took off, Divya's legs stiffened. She was glad she wasn't sitting near a window to see how far up they were. The noise inside the cockpit was deafening, and the plane bumped around like an old railcar. Her heart raced. *What am I doing?* She was about to jump out of a plane with a man she'd known for… *Had it really just been three days?* The plane lurched and her heart went with it. A light at the front of the plane turned yellow, and there were two beeps. That was their signal to get ready to jump.

I can't do this. She had taken everything too far. In her desperation to escape her wedding and her longing to sing at Café Underground, she'd completely lost her mind. What was she doing thousands of miles away from her family? How had she abandoned all her responsibilities? What was she doing sleeping with Ethan, playing with his emotions and her own? How was she pretending that this was a vacation and when it was done, everything would go back to the way things had been? That she would be the same person?

Ethan had said that if she got to a point where she really didn't want to do it, all she had to do was say the safe word, *bridesnatcher,* and they could abort.

Ethan pulled her close and she heard him attaching the harness that would connect them, just as they'd practiced on the ground. His body felt solid against hers. "The first time I did this, I was scared out of my mind, but after this, there's nothing you'll be afraid of. It's time to let go of all the fears you hold inside you."

She exhaled. "I can't do this. I can't!" But the words were stuck inside her throat.

"I've got you," he whispered in her ear. "I'll be with you." He wrapped his arms around her tightly. Her heart rate slowed. He wouldn't let anything happen to her.

The light buzzed green and he pushed her forward until they were at the door.

"Don't worry. He hasn't lost one yet," Buck quipped as Ethan opened the plane door. A rush of air assaulted them, and she was sure she'd get blown right out of the plane. She tried to find something on the floor to grab on to, but her hands were so sweaty that they just slid over the floor. Ethan stood, lifting her up with him.

She was unstable on her legs since he was taller than she was and they were now harnessed together. He held on to a strap on the ceiling with one hand and slowly shuffled them along. The cold air slammed her in the face as they got to the edge of the plane.

Her chest exploded. She was pretty sure she was having a heart attack. *Oh my God!* Wisps of white clouds froze her face and hands. She could barely see the streaks of blue below. She couldn't breathe. Her legs were so stiff, she couldn't move them. Ethan pushed her gently and her toes went over the edge of the plane. She screamed, but no sound came out of her mouth. She squeezed her eyes shut. There was no way she could do this. It was time to use the safe word and abort. She'd never been this scared in her life. Her heels were barely on the edge of the plane.

"You ready?" Ethan yelled next to her ear, and yet she could barely hear him over the rush of the wind.

He gently moved them forward, and now her feet weren't touching anything. All she felt was a tug against her harness where she was connected to Ethan. *What if he couldn't open the parachute in time?* She knew what was coming next, and that Ethan was waiting for her to use the safe word. She tried to take a breath, but she'd forgotten how to breathe. Her lungs were burning. *Bridesnatcher! Bridesnatcher!* Had she said the words out loud?

Ethan wrapped an arm around her waist and squeezed tightly. "Trust me." She took a shuddering breath, leaned forward slightly, and he pushed off with his feet. They went over the edge.

The air slapped her face and her skin felt like it would tear away. They were falling, rolling around uncontrollably, and she didn't know for a second if her heart was even beating. She was supposed to do something, but she couldn't remember what. She was going to die and kill Ethan with her because she couldn't remember the body position for the free fall.

Then Ethan grabbed her arms and thrust his body forward to force her to arch, turning them so her belly was facing the earth. Now her body was flat against the wind and she was looking straight down through the clouds. The wind rushed into her face. Her heart was beating so wildly, she could feel it in her throat. Her mouth was open, but she wasn't sure if she was actually screaming. All she could hear was the deafening sound of the wind in her ears, the sting of cold on her face and Ethan's solid body on her back.

Everywhere she looked, the color blue stretched before her; she could barely make out where the sky ended and the water began. It felt like they were in free fall forever, even though they'd told her that it would be only a minute. All of a sudden, she felt a sharp tug between her legs as the parachute opened and the harness yanked her into position.

They slowed and she gasped at the sight before her. The glimmering waters of the gulf and Atlantic stretched out endlessly. A tiny line marked US Route 1, connecting the Keys with the rest of Florida. There were tiny specks of green land dotted with what she figured were houses and businesses. It was surreal, like she was having an out-of-body experience. In that moment, nothing mattered, not her family, not the decisions that lay before her, not even her life. The world spread out beneath her, full of possibilities.

"How do you feel?" Ethan said.

She tried to turn and look at him but could see only his hands holding on to the straps of the parachute. "I feel free. Like I can do anything in the world."

She didn't need to see his face to feel his smile. "The first time I did this was when I was a senior in high school. Buck's dad owned a dive shop in Wisconsin right across the Minnesota border. He'd been doing it for years. There was this girl who I'd been in love with since ninth grade. She'd finally noticed me, and we were both headed to the same college. I knew now was the time to finally ask her out, but I was so afraid of rejection. Buck told me that after I did this, I could remember that I'd jumped out of an airplane and nothing seems scary after that."

She laughed and they both shook in the harness. She had to admit that she'd never felt her heart beat as hard as it was now.

"I hope that the next time you're afraid to do something, this experience gives you the courage to face your worst fear." His words hit her deep in her solar plexus.

As they came closer to the ground, Ethan navigated the parachute and they could see the cars on the road and the runway they had used. The plane was lifting off. There was a green field with markings, and she knew that was where they were supposed to land.

"Remember how we practiced the landing? Raise your legs now." Divya did as she was told, and it felt like the earth rushed up suddenly to meet them. But the landing was surprisingly soft. Ethan got his footing then lifted her slightly so she was also standing. The parachute floated behind them. He disconnected them and she turned and hugged him tightly.

Every cell in her body was alive in a way she'd never experienced. "Oh my God. That was the most amazing thing I've ever done in my life."

He grinned.

She stood on her toes and kissed him with everything she had. She'd just jumped out of a plane. Ethan was right: after this, there was nothing she couldn't do. He held her close as he kissed her, and this time it was more than just her body that responded to him. Her soul reached out to touch him, to thank him for giving her this experience, to tell him just how much she cared for him. It felt like they were connected at a cellular level, like he knew her better than she knew herself, and she wanted nothing more than to give herself to him entirely.

Ethan finally broke the kiss. "Divya, there's something I need to say to you."

The catch in his voice sent a chill through her. Was this it? Was he going to tell her that they were going to part ways? They hadn't discussed how long this would last, and he certainly didn't owe her anything.

He cupped her face. "I know you told me not to go for girls who are unavailable. But I can't seem to help it. I need you to know that when things end between us, I can't be friends with you."

He said when *things end between us. Not* if. He'd already given up on her.

Eleven

"I got people coming in," a man in a yellow jumpsuit yelled out to them.

"Sorry!" Ethan yelled back. What was he thinking? They had to get off the landing field. Now was not the time to kiss Divya or tell her how he felt. They went to the shack and removed their harnesses and jumpsuits.

She was silent as he motored back onto US Route 1. He would've liked to have stayed in the Keys for a couple of days, but it was his parents' anniversary. He wanted to take Divya to meet his family. But not before he told her where he stood.

That connection he'd been searching for with Pooja, the one he thought he was crazy to want, had come to him in the form of yet another woman who was totally unavailable. But he wasn't going to let her go without a fight.

He pulled onto another dirt road. "Get ready. This is going to be one of the best meals you'll ever have," he said lightly. Divya's silence was heavy in the air, but she cracked a smile as they looked up at the sign that read Joey's Love Boat.

A bar and kitchen were set up on the sandy shore. The dining room was a houseboat. A young girl wearing a tank top and shorts asked them to wait until a table opened up. There was a small beach area next to the boat, and without discussing it, they both took off their shoes and went to dip their toes in the cool water.

"What did you mean when you said we can't be friends?" she asked without preamble.

"It's exactly what you think, Divya."

He turned and put his hands on her arms. Her body softened and she moved closer to him until their noses touched. A lump formed in his throat. "You were right Divya, when it's the right person, you don't need a lot of time to know. It took Vivek three weeks to know that you were the one for him. It's only taken me three days. I love you, Divya."

She froze, then stepped back from him.

"Your table is ready." The waitress appeared, holding menus. Ethan let go of Divya and she turned away from him. His heart sank deep into his toes. This was why he'd jumped today, to find the courage to tell her how he felt. She could choose to end things now, but he didn't want to be with her unless she knew he was in it for real.

Every minute he spent with her, he knew he'd be in free fall. He wanted to know how she felt before it was too late to pull the parachute.

The hostess led them onto the boat. There were only ten tables, each covered with a colorful tablecloth and adorned with fresh flowers arranged in beer bottles.

As they sat, the boat rocked slightly, causing a little of the water the waitress had poured into their glasses to slosh over the rims. The afternoon was hot and muggy, and he noticed Divya fanning herself. "I should've warned you we were going someplace hot so you could've dressed for it."

"You should've warned me that things were going to get hot between us."

The waitress reappeared to take their orders, and Divya asked him to order for them. He ordered coconut shrimp, fresh mahi-mahi, and as the waitress was leaving, Divya asked for a rum punch.

"Need a drink, huh?" he quipped.

"We need to talk."

While a part of him had hoped she'd tell him she loved him too and was ready to be with him, he hadn't really expected it. That wasn't how things worked for him. Like everyone else in his life, she was about to reject him.

"I need to tell you the real reason I don't want to get married."

He leaned forward. Was she finally going to trust him with what she'd been holding back?

"Remember I told you about Sameer's car accident?" A lump formed in her throat and she felt the sting of tears in her eyes. "He was hurt pretty badly, but he recovered fine, or so we all thought. Then we went into lockdown, and I noticed he started acting strangely. At first, I was worried he had the virus, but when I pushed to call the family doctor, Sameer told me that he hadn't given up the pain medications from his accident. He'd been buying them illegally and couldn't get them because of the lockdown. He was in withdrawal. He didn't want the family to know, he was so ashamed."

"So you hid it from them and helped him through it." Ethan wasn't surprised that Divya had nurtured her brother through his addiction.

She nodded. "It wasn't just about protecting his health. Arjun's wife, Rani, was pregnant, and they were in Vegas for the lockdown. Sameer had taken on Arjun's business responsibilities so Arjun could focus on his family. The last thing Sameer could do was manage a multibillion-dollar empire while going through withdrawal. I was already involved in the business, so I took over his responsibilities. No one knew that I was doing his work. My family still doesn't know."

"Is Sameer still struggling?"

She nodded. "He says he's fine. He hasn't relapsed for almost six months, but in two months, we're going to be launching a new hotel in DC, and I know what the stress does to him."

"Why can't another family member help him?"

"The only person who could handle that kind of responsibility is Arjun. But he can't leave Vegas and return to India. His daughter, Simmi, was born with a heart murmur. She's had surgery, but she needs to be constantly monitored, and she can't travel. That's why my wedding was in Vegas. It would kill Arjun to leave Rani and Simmi alone."

"What about your sisters?"

"Sameer is too manipulative for my younger sisters to handle. The last time he relapsed, it took me weeks to figure it out and I was watching him like a hawk."

"So you're going to dedicate your life to helping him cope?" Ethan couldn't keep the disbelief and disappointment out of his voice, and Divya noticed. She sat up straighter.

"That's what we do for family. We take care of each other. We give up our selfish needs to help them."

Their food arrived, which saved him from saying something he'd regret.

"If something happened to Sameer, I'd never be able to live with myself," Divya said softly.

He pushed the food toward her. They dug in, ravenous after their adrenaline-filled morning.

"Sameer isn't going to need you forever," Ethan said carefully. "He will eventually kick it."

Divya dipped a coconut shrimp in pineapple salsa. "Sameer is the reason I need to return to my family right now. But it still doesn't change the fact that I don't want to spend my life on someone else's terms. My mother was twenty-three years old when she married my father. For eighteen years, ever since she was five, she'd been studying classical Indian dance. *Bharatnatyam*. It's a real art that takes decades to learn. She was so good that she earned several awards. When she married my father, she gave that all up to take care of his household and have his children. He would never let her dance publicly. I still remember when I was a little girl I'd catch her with *ghunghuru*—those are bells you wear on your feet for classical dance. She tried to hide it from me, but I'd hear the music coming from her room and the sound of the bells as she tapped her feet in perfect rhythm. When I was older, I asked her why she hid it from me, and she said it was because she didn't want me to fall in love with something I could not have."

"That's not how it is in my family," he said gently. "I would never tell my wife what she can and cannot do." She fidgeted as he said the word *wife*, and his stomach clenched. "Come with me tonight and meet my family. You'll see that we share the same family values but a very different sense of what a marriage partnership looks like. We're not as far apart as you think."

She chewed on her lip. "Are you sure?"

"It's not as big a deal in my house to bring someone home as it is in yours. We don't even have to tell them we're involved, if you don't want."

She ate in silence for a few minutes.

"I'd like to meet your family. But I don't want to hurt you."

What she meant was that she didn't want to lead him on. "I'm clear on the fact that you don't want a long-term relationship. I understand the reasons why. I may not agree, but I understand." *And I plan to change your mind.*

As they finished their meal, Ethan stole glances at

Divya. She seemed to be lost in her own world. He'd put his cards on the table. It was her turn now to decide how she wanted to proceed. She needed to figure out whether she was brave enough to love him back.

"A rupee for your thoughts."

She gave him a small smile. "Boy, you're cheap. Not even a whole dollar?"

He took the last piece of the coconut shrimp, dipped it and held it out to her. She leaned forward and took the bite directly from his hand, flicking her tongue to lick the sauce off his fingers. He rubbed his thumb on her lips, then touched her cheek.

"I don't want to say goodbye to you, Ethan."

You say that Divya, but are you going to break my heart like the rest of them?

Twelve

It was dusk by the time they arrived in Minneapolis. A Lexus sedan was waiting for them at the airport, with a big bow on top of it.

"It's a present for my parents." Ethan grinned. "My mom's car is on its last legs."

Divya pressed her lips together.

"What is it? I know you want to say something."

She sighed. "You said your parents don't like accepting help from you. Isn't this a little extravagant?"

He waved her off as he loaded their luggage and the gift bags Roda had given him in New York into the trunk. "It's an anniversary present."

There was some traffic as they got onto the highway. "My parents are in Stillwater. When we have time tomorrow, I'll show you the town. It's really cute with antiques shops, riverboats and even a park with a giant teddy bear." He loved taking his niece and nephew to Teddy Bear Park. He'd been sad when they'd outgrown it. Lately he'd had trouble connecting with them, like he used to when they were much younger and all it took to make them happy was a game of peekaboo or a ride on his shoulders. But he was hoping that the gifts he'd bought would help return his cool-uncle status. His chest constricted as he thought about how much he'd loved the baby phase with all of the kids. As they'd grown, he'd looked forward to reliving each part of their childhood with his own children.

He snuck a look at Divya. *Why do I keep doing this to myself?*

Traffic was light as he got on the highway. Was he doing the right thing, taking Divya to meet his family? He wanted her to see the love he had for them, to know that he understood her commitment to her own family. They weren't as different as she thought.

His parents lived in an old neighborhood. When he was growing up, it had been small houses like his own, with large backyards full of children. After a few large companies had opened headquarters close to the community, the home prices had gone through the roof. By the time he was in middle school, the older houses had been torn down and replaced with towering mansions with private swimming pools and tennis courts. His parents' house stuck out like a sore thumb in the neighborhood, but his father refused to sell or renovate. He wanted to keep it exactly as it was, and Ethan was secretly glad.

As he passed a particular redbrick house with a white picket fence, he slowed down like he always did. But this time he also found himself stepping on the brake, reversing back and pulling into the driveway.

"Are your parents not home? The house is dark."

"This isn't my parents' house."

She looked at him questioningly.

"It's my house. Or I should say, a house I bought."

She leaned over and placed a hand on his arm.

"Houses rarely come up for sale in this neighborhood, and my father is never selling his, so I bought it to be close to them. But I never moved in. They don't even know I own it."

"Why didn't you tell them?"

He shrugged. "I bought the place right after Pooja left me and I didn't want to hear my parents tell me that I'd made another mistake."

He reversed the car and drove back onto the road, his throat tight. Why had he shown it to Divya? The only person who knew he owned it was his accountant. Was he being impulsive in loving her? Did he want to fill this house so badly that he was clinging to whoever came his way? He took a breath to ease the constriction in his chest.

As the car crunched over the gravel driveway of his parents' house, Ethan relaxed. The sight of the gray siding, stone chimney and the two rocking chairs on the front porch filled him with comforting warmth. The house had looked this way all his life. No matter how hard a day he'd had at school, when the bus had dropped him off at the end of the street, he'd looked forward to walking up the porch steps. He parked beside his mother's old car so she wouldn't see the Lexus's bow from the front porch. He couldn't wait to give this gift to her.

His mother came outside to meet them. She looked the same as always, dressed in jeans and a knitted sweater. She was a small woman, no more than five foot four with blond hair and tired blue eyes, which reminded him of the fact that she still put in long hours at the diner. He enveloped her in a bear hug.

"It is good to see you, my boy." She hugged him back, holding on to him tightly and making him feel like everything was okay with the world. "I thought you'd forgotten."

He kissed her on the cheek. "Happy anniversary."

"Who's this?" She looked at Divya.

"Mom, meet Divya."

Divya held out her hand, but his mother leaned in and gave her a hug. "Welcome."

Ethan surreptitiously removed their bags from the car, and Divya retrieved the pie she'd insisted on picking up and handed it to Marilyn.

"Now, what's this?"

"Key lime pie from the Florida Keys," Divya replied.

His mother's eyes widened. "Now, that's mighty thoughtful of you. Well, come on in, Bill is probably wondering what's taking us so long."

They walked into a small foyer that led to a staircase to the second floor and a dining room on the right. Divya followed Marilyn into the kitchen, where

Ethan's dad stood to greet them. He had dark hair and gray eyes. He was a thin man with round glasses and a goatee.

"It's nice to meet you, Mr. Connors," Divya said.

"Oh, call me Bill."

"Divya brought a pie for us from the Keys," Marilyn said as she set the pie down.

"Wow." Bill looked at the pie as if he was making sure it was real.

"What were you guys doing in the Keys?" Bill asked.

"Ethan took me skydiving."

Marilyn shot Bill a look that didn't escape Ethan's notice. When he'd been a kid, he'd hated how his parents communicated wordlessly; now he compared every one of his relationships to that connection they had.

"Matt and the kids should be here any minute. I made pot roast." Marilyn looked at Divya. "Are you okay with that?"

"I've never had pot roast, so I'd love to try it."

"Mom makes the best pot roast." Ethan leaned over and gave his mother an affectionate kiss. "I've been looking forward to it for weeks." Marilyn leaned over and tousled his hair.

"So are you and Divya sharing a bedroom?" Marilyn asked.

Divya looked down and Ethan enjoyed seeing the twinge of color on her cheeks.

"Um, no, we're not staying in the same room," Divya said.

"We're not?" Ethan whispered to her and she shot him a look.

Marilyn looked between them and rolled her eyes. "Ethan, why don't you show Divya to your room and I'll make up the couch in the family room for you."

Ethan carried her bag upstairs and she followed.

"Is this your childhood room?"

He nodded, looking at the familiar space. The walls were covered with Star Wars posters. The bookshelf held the memorabilia he'd brought home from college. He knew every inch of this room. One of the first things he and Bill had done together was put the bed together. This had been Bill's office before he'd married his mom.

Ethan reached to the back of the bookshelf and pulled out a framed photo. It pictured a younger version of Marilyn, Wade and Ethan, when he was about four.

"That's your real father?" Divya asked.

"Bill is my real father. This is the man who cheated on my mother, drank himself into a stupor every night and took five seconds to sign away his paternity rights."

She placed her hand on his chest, her eyes shining. He lifted her hand and kissed it. "Don't feel sorry for this poor little rich boy. Bill loves my mom and he's been a wonderful father. It could've turned out very differently for me."

"I hope you know that your father rejecting you had nothing to do with you and everything to do with him."

Ethan nodded. "I know that at some level. But he

wasn't always a drunk. Mom told me his drinking started after I was born."

"You didn't drive him to drink."

"I know." He hadn't looked at the picture in years, but he'd needed to show it to Divya, to have her understand that there was a reason he ran scared from relationships. But that he was ready to confront his demons, just like he'd asked her to confront hers.

"Not a lot of people know this, but Arjun is my half brother. My dad had a first wife who died when Arjun was a baby. We never knew. We found out a few years ago, and Arjun was devastated. For the rest of us, it didn't matter. He had always been our big brother and would still be. Nothing changed for us. But he started treating us differently. It was him that put distance between us because he felt like he didn't belong."

"You think that's what I'm doing?"

"I think it's time for you to realize that you're a wonderful man and there's nothing wrong with you."

He ran his hands down the length of her arms, feeling the goose bumps, and placed a light kiss on her lips. Then moved on to her neck. She brushed her hair aside and tilted her head. He'd been with a number of women in his life, but it felt different with Divya. As aroused as he was, he was also content just being close to her, touching her skin, smelling her sweet vanilla scent.

He circled her waist with his arm and pulled her closer. He untucked her silk shirt and ran his hands underneath it to cup her breasts, enjoying how perfectly they fit in his hands and how taut her nipples became at his slightest touch.

"Matt's here." Marilyn's voice came clear up the stairs, and Divya pushed Ethan away. He smirked.

"Coming, Mom." Divya quickly tucked her shirt back in and adjusted her bra. He leaned in close to her ear, kissing the lobe while whispering, "Don't worry, we'll pick it up tonight. The bed is really comfortable."

Her eyes widened. "We're not having sex."

He raised his brows. "Then, what did we do on the plane?"

She shook her head. "I mean we're not having sex here. It wouldn't be proper in your parents' house."

"You're kidding, right? They know I have sex. I'm sure my mom thinks it's silly you want me to sleep on the couch."

"But it's not okay by me."

"You're serious?"

She nodded. Marilyn called out to Ethan again. They went downstairs to see his brother's minivan in the driveway. The kids, Allie and Jake, burst out of the back, slamming the door shut in their excitement to give Ethan a hug. He held them close in a group hug, his heart overflowing with love for them.

"Uncle Ethan, you won't believe what happened at school today." He turned his full attention to five-year-old Jake, who had his mother's dark hair and brown eyes. Jake went on to give him the lowdown on the most recent recess games.

"That's enough, Jake, Uncle Ethan doesn't need to hear everything that happens in kindergarten." Allie was seven going on fifteen. She was the perfect mix of her mom and dad with platinum blond hair from Bill's side and big eyes and a snub nose from Heather.

"Nice to see you again, Ethan."

He smiled at his sister-in-law. She had dark hair, brown eyes and a tall, slim build. She was holding two covered dishes. "You okay?" he asked, taking them from her. Heather looked tired.

She gave him a small smile. "Just the usual grind, dealing with these kids." She shot them an affectionate glance.

His brother came up and gave him a hug. Every time he saw his brother, it always surprised him that Matt was no longer the small, lanky boy from Ethan's memory. He was as tall as Ethan but with a much stockier build. Ethan slapped his younger brother on the back. It was hard to see Matt with kids of his own. Ethan still remembered the day his mother came home from the hospital with newborn Matt bundled in her arms. Ethan had stood at the top of the stairs and watched his parents become a family. And then twenty years later, he'd watched Heather and Matt become a family.

"Why does that car have a bow?" Allie asked.

Ethan grinned. He'd been hoping to wait until the morning when he could show them the car, but now was as good a time as any. "It's Mom and Dad's anniversary present."

Marilyn gasped. "Ethan! What're we going to do with a car like that?"

"Get rid of your old beater and not worry about car repairs."

Bill put a hand on Ethan's shoulders. "Thanks, son.

This is mighty generous of you, but we're doing fine. This is too much—we don't need it."

Ethan clenched his jaw. "It's your wedding anniversary. I have the right to buy my parents a gift, don't I?"

"We bought them a bottle of wine," Matt said unhelpfully.

"Why don't we go inside and set the table," Heather said and took the kids inside. Matt and Divya followed.

"Come on, Mom. Accept this. For me." Ethan put on his most charming smile and put his arm around his mom. "It'll make me so happy to see you enjoy a luxury for once."

Marilyn shook her head. "I appreciate it, Ethan, but this isn't for me. I'm used to my old clunker."

"I don't understand why you guys don't like nice things," Ethan said with obvious impatience. "I know you think my money is easy, but I earn it honestly. What's wrong with me wanting to spend it on the people I love, to give you nice things?"

"We don't need it, son," Bill said firmly. "I can take care of my family."

My family. Bill's family. Blood pounded inside his ears. It had always been like that. While Bill called him *son*, the fact that Ethan was in truth his stepson was always just under the surface in their family. He would always be the boy looking down from the staircase.

"Fine. I'll take the car back." Ethan took a breath as he walked into the house and to the backyard, where Divya was helping Heather set the table.

Jake came running toward him, and Ethan scooped him up. He was getting too big to really carry, but

Ethan couldn't resist. He'd seen how fast Allie had grown up.

"Uncle Ethan, where's that Poo lady?"

Ethan caught Divya's eyes and saw that she was barely suppressing a laugh at Jake's question.

"Her name was Pooja and she won't be coming around anymore, buddy," Ethan answered. He set Jake down and the boy went in search of a soccer ball.

"Exactly how many women do you bring home?" Divya said, her voice weirdly high. He turned to her, ready to make a snarky comment, but the look in her eyes stopped him. He didn't want to tell her what he told his family each time he brought home a new woman: that he wanted them to see that he came from humble beginnings.

He put his arm around her waist and pulled her close. "It helps to have someone in my corner."

Divya gave him a kiss, and he was grateful he didn't need to say any more, that he didn't need to verbalize his insecurities. He knew from the look in her eyes that she understood.

"Did you bring us anything, Uncle Ethan?"

Ethan disentangled himself from Divya and looked affectionately at Allie. He'd had Roda pick up the latest iPhone for his niece and a gaming console for Jake. He still remembered being the kid at school who didn't have the coolest new toy.

"Of course I've got something for you." He gave them the gift bags Roda had handed him in New York. The kids excitedly opened them and squealed in delight as they found their requested items. "You are the best, Uncle Ethan." Jake beamed.

Allie screamed. "Oh my God, my friends are going to die when they see I have this."

"Ethan, we've talked about the expensive gifts." Matt's weary voice broke into the kids' excited chatter. When the kids were out of earshot, examining their toys, Matt turned to him. "Ethan, you've got to stop buying them such expensive things."

Ethan rubbed his neck. "I'm their uncle, I have the right to spoil them."

Matt exchanged a look with Heather, who shook her head imperceptibly at him, and he turned away from Ethan. Ethan looked to his parents for support, but they were exchanging glances of their own. Ethan's breath stuck. Then he felt Divya's hand on his arm.

"You've got me in your corner," she whispered.

Thirteen

Marilyn broke the tension by asking everyone to come to the outdoor table for dinner. Divya had watched the exchange with Ethan's parents and then his brother, and her heart ached for him. He was trying so hard to find his place, his role in the family, and he was doing it all wrong. He thought he could do it by being the rich uncle who spoiled the kids and provided for everyone.

The conversation at dinner was easy as the kids excitedly filled them in on the happenings at school. Ethan engaged in genuine conversation with the kids. He knew the names of their friends and their favorite teachers, and even the supersecret code name of the boy Allie liked but her parents didn't know about. They asked Divya about herself, and what it was like living in India.

It was exactly the kind of dinner her family had when they were together. There was a lot of laughter and good-natured ribbing, and the love was palpable across the table.

"Marilyn, can you pick up the kids from school tomorrow? I have to work late and Matt has a PTA meeting," Heather said.

"What's a PTA?" Divya asked.

"Parent Teacher Association," Heather responded. "Matt volunteers as the room parent for the kids."

Divya raised her eyebrows. "Most of my friends have kids, and I don't think a single one of their husbands volunteers at the school."

Heather smiled and leaned over to kiss Matt. "He is an amazing guy. When we had Allie, I was in medical school. I couldn't postpone residency, so he stayed home with Allie. Now I'm doing my surgical fellowship and my schedule is crazy. There's no way I could do it if it weren't for Matt."

"So you gave up your career for her?" Divya slapped her hand to her mouth as soon as she said the words. She hadn't meant to sound so incredulous.

Matt smiled. "I'm an accountant. I do some consulting on the side to keep up my skills. When the kids are a little older, I can easily go back to my job. It's much harder for Heather to take a break in her medical training. This is the time to focus on Heather's career."

Divya couldn't imagine her father saying something like that. She almost laughed at the thought of her father giving up his career so her mother could become a dancer. She looked at Ethan and pictured him in the audience cheering for her at Café Underground.

"Anyway, can you pick them up?" Heather asked Marilyn.

Ethan's mother sighed. "I'm sorry. I have a double shift."

"We can do it," Divya piped up.

Ethan looked at her in surprise but then chimed in, "Yeah, in fact we will pick them up and feed them dinner if you and Matt want an evening to yourselves."

Everyone looked at him in surprise. Heather and Matt exchanged a look.

"Mom, can we, please?" Jake said excitedly.

"Sounds like a great idea," Marilyn said.

"It's a very nice offer." Heather looked at Ethan and then Divya. "Are you sure?"

They both nodded enthusiastically, and under the table, Ethan squeezed Divya's hand. The kids whooped and began discussing where they wanted to go eat the next day.

Divya excused herself to go get a jacket. The evening was getting chilly for her, especially after the hot day in the Keys. As she came down the stairs, she heard Marilyn and Matt talking in the kitchen.

"You need to talk to him, Mom. A week ago, he told me he wished he'd proposed to Pooja, and now he's here with someone else. I don't know what's going on with him."

His mother sighed. "He's so damn impulsive. I knew Pooja would never marry him. The last time she was here, she pretty much told me that her parents would never accept someone who wasn't Indian. I swear, he purposely picks women who're going to break his heart."

"You know he met Divya while trying to crash Pooja's wedding? I saw it on social media. Divya was marrying someone else four days ago and got cold feet. I'm worried about him, Mom. I don't want to see him get hurt. It's obvious he cares about her."

Marilyn sighed. "He's been like this all his life. I don't know whether he's faster at falling in love or out of it. I'll try talking to him tomorrow."

Divya's stomach dropped. Marilyn had just put into words the thing she feared the most. When Ethan told her he loved her, she wanted nothing more than to say it back to him. To tell him that she had been picturing what it'd be like to introduce him to her family, to have him dress up in an Indian *sherwani* and celebrate the upcoming Diwali holidays with them. She had started thinking of things that she'd never considered before. But she'd never told anyone she'd loved them. Not even Vivek. The best she'd been able to tell him was "ditto" when he'd said it to her, and she hadn't truly meant it. For her, love was something that happened once in a lifetime. With someone that made her heart explode. That someone was Ethan. But she didn't want to be yet another girl that he was in free fall with. He'd said that he expected her to break his heart, but somehow she knew he'd be the one shattering hers.

She heard plates clinking, then the door open and close. She waited a few more minutes, then quietly slipped back into the backyard.

"Wow, this pie is amazing, where did you get it?" Heather exclaimed.

"Divya brought it from the Florida Keys."

"Mmm, why haven't you brought this for us before, Ethan?" Matt cut himself another piece. "Did you take her skydiving with Buck?" The way he said it, Divya got the feeling that it was something Ethan did all the time. Maybe it was his standard date for all those girls he'd fallen in love with.

Everyone pitched in to clear the table, and Divya liked the easy way they worked together. The kids carried the plates to the kitchen while Marilyn and Heather packed up the leftovers, and Matt, Ethan and Bill moved the extra dining room chairs back inside. Divya stood back and watched, listening to their banter, watching Ethan light up from the inside.

Matt, Heather and the kids left to get the kids to bed. Ethan began loading the dishwasher, and Bill wiped down the kitchen counters.

"Coffee, Divya? Or do you prefer tea?"

"Whatever you're having."

Marilyn started the coffeemaker. Divya watched Ethan load the dishwasher, arguing with his dad about the best way to position the dishes. Her brother Arjun liked to cook, but she'd never seen him clean. Rani was working hard to teach him how to wash dishes. Divya and her siblings had grown up with servants who did the cleaning after family meals, under her mother's supervision while her father and brothers retired to the living room for a nightcap.

Marilyn handed Divya a coffee cup, and they went to the front porch and sat in the rocking chairs.

"You know, I really don't mind you and Ethan sleeping in the same room," Marilyn said.

Divya's cheeks burned. "My parents are very old-fashioned. It wouldn't feel right."

Marilyn smiled. "I can tell your mother raised you well. Thank you helping with the kids tomorrow."

"It's my pleasure. They seem wonderful." Divya meant it. Two of her closest friends were married with kids, and while she adored her pseudo nieces and nephews, they were spoiled. Matt's kids seemed to be well-grounded, the way she'd like to raise her own kids. The thought stopped her cold. Why was she thinking about children?

Marilyn looked toward the Lexus with the bow on it. "I don't know what Ethan was thinking with that car."

Divya bit her lip. She hadn't heard the full exchange between Ethan and his parents regarding the car, but from the face he carried with him to dinner, she knew they'd rejected it, just as she'd suspected they would. It wasn't her place to say anything but what did she have to lose? It wasn't as if she was trying to impress his parents or audition for the role of his wife. She might as well help him as a friend.

"You know, he was really excited to give you the car. It would mean a lot to him if you'd accept it."

"I don't know how many times we've tried to explain to Ethan that we don't want money or gifts, and yet he doesn't seem to get it," Marilyn said irritably.

Divya's heart clenched. "Do you know that during the pandemic, he donated most of the money he earned to people who had lost their jobs and healthcare workers? He still pays the salaries of those employees who died from the virus or can no longer work so their families are okay. He goes around giving ridiculous tips. He's not like the other billionaires in the world who spend their money buying mansions." Her voice nearly cracked as she thought about how excited he'd been to give his mother the car. "He's not trying to throw his money around. He feels lucky to have it and wants to share it with the people he loves most."

Marilyn blew out a breath. "We don't want to hurt his feelings. It's just that the money seems to have changed him. He used to take the kids to the park, and now he wants to take them to Paris and London. That's not how I raised my boys, and it's not how Matt wants to raise his kids."

Divya chewed on her lip. She didn't know Ethan's parents and maybe she should keep her mouth shut and stay out of the whole situation. "Ethan loves the way he grew up. This is not about passing judgment on what you weren't able to give him. The money is meaningless to him unless he can enjoy it with you. When you don't accept his gifts, it makes him feel like he's not a part of this family."

Marilyn stared at Divya and she shifted in her seat.

"You and Ethan really only met a few days ago?"

Divya nodded.

"Then, how is it that you know my son so well?"

Divya shrugged. "Maybe because we met each other

at a vulnerable time, or maybe because we're going to be together for such a short time, we don't feel the need for any pretenses between us."

Marilyn sipped her coffee. "Maybe we've been hard on Ethan. But the money seemed to change him overnight. He was never into private jets and luxury condos."

"I have never had pot roast, but after dinner tonight, I'm going to want to learn how to make it." Divya warmed her hands on the coffee mug. "I've been around spoiled rich men all my life. Ethan is not one of them. He'd give away all his money if that's what it would take for things to be right with you."

They sat in companionable silence, drinking their coffees, then Marilyn reached out her hand and patted Divya's. "You're a good girl, Divya. I hope you're not just around for a short time."

Divya dropped her gaze to the coffee cup. She tried to imagine Marilyn with her well-worn sweater and jeans sitting next to her own mother, who was always in designer clothes. She couldn't. Nor could she imagine Ethan sitting with her father in his study, dressed in a *kurta pajama*, with a crystal tumbler of whiskey.

Ethan's parents retired to their bedroom and Divya joined Ethan on the couch in the family room. He turned off the TV. "Are you tired?"

"It's only nine o'clock. This is usually when we eat dinner at my house," Divya said.

He shrugged. "My mom is usually up early to get to the diner before breakfast is served, so we've always been an early-to-bed household." He put his arm around her and she snuggled into him, enjoying the warmth of his body. "Thanks for breaking the tension with my brother. You don't have to babysit tomorrow. I can take care of it."

She touched his arm. "They seem like nice kids. I'd like to get to know them." And she meant it.

"I don't know why my brother has such a chip on his shoulder about me getting them expensive presents. Heather has some serious medical-school loans to pay off, and she's still in training, so she doesn't make that much money. With Matt not working, I know he can't afford that stuff. I'm only trying to help," Ethan said wearily.

She sighed. "My college friend has a five-year-old who I love to spoil. She asked me to stop buying him expensive presents because it undermines what she and her husband can provide for him. It's hard for them that he has a rich auntie. Think of how your brother must feel about the fact that his kids are more excited about what you give them with your spare change than what he sacrifices every day to provide for them. It's hard being the parent who has to buy clothes and books, while you get to swoop in and be the hero giving them cool toys. If you want to help, ask your brother what he needs for the kids. Give them the things they need every day."

Ethan rolled his head back and closed his eyes. She reached over and rubbed her thumbs over his forehead.

"Hmm. Is that a head massage?"

"Kind of. My mom does it when I'm stressed and angry. It calms me down."

He smiled. "It's working." He grabbed her hand and kissed her fingers. "You know, there's something else that would be really de-stressing right now."

She pulled her hands back. "Oh no, you're not tempting me into doing *that* in your parents' house."

He pulled her close to him. "They sleep really soundly." He turned her hand and kissed the inside of her wrist, then began working his way up her arm. Delicious tingles worked their way from his mouth all the way to her core.

She pulled her arm back. "How about we watch a movie?"

He let out a sigh of frustration but grabbed the remote. She placed her head on his chest, enjoying the warmth of his body and the steady beat of his heart. She was asleep before the movie even started.

She woke when she felt him carrying her up the stairs to the bedroom. He set her gently on the bed, gave her a kiss on the forehead, placed the blankets on her and left the room. After he'd left, she sat up and turned on the light. There was little furniture in the room, just a bed, nightstand and a bookshelf that held a picture of two young boys with their arms around each other, grinning widely. She picked it up. It reminded her of a photo at home of her and her three sisters, all with the same pigtails and school uniforms. Her heart clenched painfully. *What am I doing here?* She was in Minnesota, a state she hadn't even known existed a few days ago, with a family that wasn't hers and a man who made her body sing in ways it never had before and had wormed his way into her heart when she'd least expected it.

Seeing Ethan with his family just made her miss hers even more. She clicked on the phone Ethan had given her. She opened her email. There were several messages from him, her sisters and one from Sameer. Her pulse quickened as she clicked on his message.

Yo sis! Cool move. I'm pretty sure this trumps all the idiot things I've ever done. Passing my bad boy trophy to you. I'm doing well. Stay away as long as you need. You deserve a break. I'm good. Really.

PS—Vivek is a *maha* bore. Why did you ever want to marry him?

She laughed and read the message several times before deciding Sameer really was okay. The messages from Arjun and her sisters weren't as comforting. Her parents were taking things really hard. Arjun begged her to come back and promised that he would make sure she didn't have to marry anyone she didn't want to. He'd gotten rid of Vivek. There was also an email from her best friend, Hema, telling her how much she missed her. Her sisters had written long messages that spanned pages. Divya closed her eyes, unable to read them.

It was time to go home.

Ethan was not real. He was a fantasy, just like her singing career. What would life be like as a singer? It would be like the last four days. Going from one place to another, with no tether to home. Having to dance on-stage wearing skimpy clothes. Maybe she'd been pursuing the wrong goals. She'd thought that knowing she had done something on her own, a success her parents hadn't bought for her, would be enough. It would fulfill her, close the hole she'd felt in her soul. But then why did she still feel so empty? Why were her thoughts full of an American man with bright blue eyes and sandy-brown hair who owned a house down the street from his parents? A world away from everyone she loved. She lay on the bed but hardly slept.

She was not going to be the woman who would make the dark, empty, redbrick house a home for him.

Fourteen

Ethan rolled his shoulders and stretched his back. The old couch had lived its life. He was tempted to order a new one, but Divya's words came back to him.

"Coffee, hon?"

He nodded to his mother, who poured him a cup and set it on the small kitchen table. It was still early in the morning, but his father had already left for work. His mother was in her diner uniform and Ethan bit his tongue to keep from asking when she'd quit.

"You know the old McPherson house?"

She looked at him, puzzled, and sat at the table, after putting a plate with eggs, toast and bacon in front of him. She'd gotten up earlier than usual to make him breakfast.

"I bought it."

She gasped. "That was you? The neighbors were wondering who the mysterious buyer was. Why didn't you tell us?"

He shrugged. "I felt silly, buying that big old house for just me. I thought I'd tell you about it when I was ready to start a family."

Marilyn hugged her son. "You don't need a woman to start a family. We are your family."

"Then, why does is feel like I can't do anything right lately?" He reached out and took his mom's hands and she squeezed his.

She smiled sadly at him. "Oh Ethan, we love you so much. We're still getting used to your money. I guess we don't want to take advantage of your generosity. Your dad and I have always provided for our children, and we're not used to the idea of our children taking responsibility for our needs."

"There's something I want to tell you," Ethan started. It was time he told his mother what he knew. "Right after Matt was born, I went to see Wade, in our old apartment."

His mother froze, but he continued. "I needed to know why he gave me up so easily. I know he wasn't a good man, but I was his son." He paused and took a sip of his coffee. "He told me that Bill only agreed to adopt me because you made it a condition of your marriage."

His mother gasped audibly. "That awful man. How dare he say something like that to you?" She grabbed Ethan's hand. "Is that what you've thought all these years? Why didn't you say something?" She shook her head. "It's not true. I never asked Bill to take you in. He fell in love with you the first time he met you. Remember that day I took you to the park?"

Ethan did remember the day. Bill had shown him how to ride his bike without the training wheels on.

"Bill proposed to me the next day. I still joke with him that he only married me because he wanted you. Oh honey, I wish you hadn't kept this in your heart all these years." His mother leaned over and gave him a hug and he hugged her back.

They sat in silence for a while, eating breakfast, then his mother turned to him. "I guess I could use a new car."

His heart soared, but before he could say something, she held up a finger. "But, I want to go down to the used car lot and pick out something safe and sturdy." Her eyes softened. "I'm sure the Lexus is amazing, but I wouldn't feel comfortable in it."

He nodded. "Anything you want, Mom. How about I pick you up when you get your break between shifts, and we'll go down together."

She stood and put her coffee cup in the sink. "About Divya…"

He stared at his plate, ready to hear the litany of things that were wrong with her. "That girl has a good head on her shoulders. She's a keeper."

He looked at his mother in surprise. She came over to him and kissed him on the head. "But prepare yourself, my boy. She's going to break your heart."

There it was. The alarm that had been blaring in his mind, that he kept silencing.

He poured a second cup of coffee and went to wake Divya. He knocked on his bedroom door, but there was no answer. He opened it to see her curled up in his bed, her dark hair across her face.

She is so beautiful.

He imagined the master bedroom in the redbrick house and waking up next to her each morning, and he couldn't. She didn't belong in that house. She didn't want the life he did.

She stirred and he brushed her hair from her face. Her eyes blinked open. "Hey there, handsome."

He smiled. "Morning, beautiful."

"Did I sleep in late?"

He shook his head, then bent down to kiss her. She wrapped her arms around him and he inhaled her smell. He moved his mouth to her ear, then her throat and then worked his way down her body.

"Wait. Your parents!"

He had made his way down to her stomach and started taking her pajamas off. "They're gone. The house is empty. You're mine," he growled.

He made love to her slowly, savoring every inch of her body, enjoying the way she responded to him, her moans music to his ears.

When they were done, he lay down beside her and pulled her close. "Well, you can wake me up that way anytime," she murmured as she laid her head on his chest.

"Can I?"

She turned her head so she could face him. "Can you what?"

"Can I wake you this way not just for the next few days but for longer?"

She sat up, grabbed a pillow and smacked him in the chest. He sat up, startled. "Did I or did I not tell you not to fall for me?" she said indignantly.

He caught the pillow and pulled her toward him. "Didn't we discuss the fact that I have a knack for falling for unavailable women?"

Her smiled faltered. "You know we're all wrong for each other."

He took the pillow from her hand and kissed her. "I know. But that's why it feels so right between us."

She put her cheek on his naked chest. "I want to be with you," she said softly. "Can you give me some time to figure things out?"

It was the best he was going to get, and he was going to take it.

He took Divya on a riverboat ride in the morning, then dropped her at the main street in Stillwater so she could explore the antiques shops. He picked up his mom at the diner during her break and convinced her to buy a fairly new Honda Accord at the used-car dealer.

Then he went to collect Divya.

"Let's have lunch at your mother's diner," Divya suggested.

"You know what? It's a great idea." He'd never brought anyone he was dating to the diner; he usually took them to the fancier restaurants in Minneapolis.

The look in his mother's eyes when he sat down in

her section with Divya made his heart burst. She didn't have to say it. She'd been waiting for him to make this move for years. His mother introduced him with pride to the regular customers, who had no idea who he was. This was the working class of Stillwater, not the people who lived in the mansions. He shook hands, listened to advice about how to be a good son and admonishments that his mother was too old to work at the diner and he should help out more. He smiled and nodded, and his mother beamed with pride.

"What should we do with the kids this afternoon?" Divya asked when they were done with lunch.

"Let's not plan anything. We can ask them what they want to do."

They picked up the kids from school and Jake asked if they could go to Teddy Bear Park. Allie rolled her eyes, but once they got to the park, Ethan noticed her climbing the giant teddy bear while he and Divya chased Jake around the obstacle course. They all climbed on the bear when it was time to leave and had someone take a picture of them.

After dinner, they bought giant ice-cream cones and made a mess trying to finish them before they melted. Ethan savored every second of the day.

When they dropped off the kids, they hugged Divya for a long time. "You'll come back, won't you, Divya? You won't be like that Poo lady?" Jake asked in a voice so sweet that Ethan's heart lurched.

Divya got on her knees so she was eye to eye with Jake. "I'm going to do my best, little man, but I can't make any promises. Remember, I live in India, that country far away."

Tears sprung to Jake's eyes. "So this is the last time we'll see each other?" He put his little arms around Divya and buried his face in her neck.

She looked at Ethan helplessly. The kids had fallen in love with Divya, just as he had. "Jake, how about I promise that we will video chat? And I can't promise when, but one day, I'll come see you."

He held out his hand and she shook it. "It's a deal," Jake said, nodding importantly.

Ethan's throat closed. When she didn't come back, it wouldn't be just his heart that was broken.

When they got back to his brother's house, Ethan asked to have a private word with Matt and Heather. Divya volunteered to tuck the kids into bed. He sat with his brother and sister-in-law for a long time, and Divya waited patiently. Once he was done, he drove Divya to the riverfront and they walked along the bank, enjoying the cool air. He held her hand. "Thank you, Divya," he said.

She turned to him surprised. "What for?"

"For showing me what I'm really looking for in a woman. All my life, I've been chasing women who do things the way I do, who think the way I do, who want the things I want. But that's not what I need. I need someone who tells me what I'm doing wrong. Who shows me a better way."

She leaned over and kissed him. "Is your plane available tomorrow?"

He smiled. "At your service. Where do you want to go? What's next on your bucket list?"

"No more bucket list. It's time for me to return to my family."

Fifteen

His face crumpled. *Should I let him suffer?* She leaned over and whispered in his ear. "I want you to come with me. I think you should meet my family."

"Did I hear you correctly?" he asked breathlessly.

She'd made the decision to go home last night. She'd been afraid of what she'd be facing when she returned, of going back to a life she didn't want. But then she thought about jumping out of the plane. Of the raw fear she'd experienced standing on the edge. If she could do that, couldn't she tell her parents that she didn't want the life that they'd chosen for her?

She'd fallen asleep thinking about how to tell Ethan that she was ready to return. And extract a promise from him that they'd continue seeing each other. Not as friends but as lovers. But then she'd spent the whole night imagining herself in her bed at home, alone. It wasn't fair to him, or to her. If she wasn't willing to give him up, then she had to go all in. She had to see whether their love could withstand the ultimate test: her parents.

She bit his ear playfully. "Yes, Ethan Connors. Look, I'm not saying I'm ready for a permanent commitment."

"Then, what are you saying?"

"I'm saying that I am willing to admit to my parents that I've fallen in love with a most unsuitable boy. I'm willing to see where things go with us. But I'm not ready to move into a redbrick house and have three-point-five kids. Can you accept that?"

His eyes shone and her chest constricted. "We can negotiate the number. I'd be happy with two-point-two-five kids."

She slapped his chest playfully and he caught her hand. "There's a lot that I'm willing to do for you, Divya. All those women I chased… I wasn't going to give up what I wanted for them. I didn't love them enough."

She'd come to the same conclusion, but she wasn't sure if he was really willing to give up his dreams for her, either.

"I took your advice and asked Matt if there was anything the kids needed," he continued, seeming to change the subject as he brushed an errant hair out of her face. "Heather is pregnant. She's still early and they haven't told my parents. It wasn't planned and they're freaking out." A small note of pride crept into his voice at the notion that he'd been trusted with something so personal. "They admitted that their house is getting really small for them. They only have one bathroom upstairs, and it's getting hard for them to share it with the kids. There's no bedroom for another child. With the school pick-up and drop-off schedules and after-school activities, and now a baby, Matt can't go back to work. They'd pay so much in babysitters that it's not worth it for him. Heather has these massive student loans from college and medical school, and it'll be a while before she starts making real money. They can't afford to buy a bigger house right now."

"I think it's great that your brother takes on the parenting responsibilities."

Ethan pulled her closer. "I would do that for you in a heartbeat." She had no doubt he would.

"So will they take money from you?"

"I'm not giving them money."

She raised her brows.

"I gave them the redbrick house."

She gasped. "Your house?"

Ethan took both her hands in his. "It was never my house. It was a dream. It's not a house you want. It's not the life you want. And I want you."

Tears stung her eyes. "I love you, Ethan." Her voice was thick and her heart swelled in her chest. She didn't know when or how she'd fallen in love with the most improbable man, but she knew it was true.

He cupped her face. "I love you, Divya. More than anything else in this world."

The kiss they shared was sweet and salty. She didn't know if the tears were hers or his.

"Before we go back to your family, can you give me a day?"

She narrowed her eyes. "Only if you tell me what we're doing. I don't want to go mountain climbing or helicopter skiing or some other crazy sport."

"You didn't enjoy the skydiving?"

She raised her chin. "I didn't say that."

He leaned down. "Then, trust me."

She smirked at him but felt her nerves ignite at the prospect of whatever he had planned and another uncomplicated day with him.

They left early the next morning. Marilyn and Bill both gave Divya a long hug and extracted a promise that she would stay in touch. Ethan slowed down as he passed by the redbrick house but resolutely refused to look at it. Divya's heart squeezed painfully.

He took them to Los Angeles and her curiosity was peaked. Yet another assistant met them, this time with a limo and driver. "LA traffic can be horrendous, and I want to make the most of our time together."

Why was he talking as if it was their last day together? He still wouldn't tell her where they were going, but according to the GPS, the ride would take over an hour, so they chatted about her family.

"Karishma is my partner in crime. She and I are only two years apart, so we've always gotten into trouble together. Naina is a little younger, so we usually con her into covering for us, but she's been getting smarter about wanting to be part of the fun."

"Did they know you were planning to run?"

"Karishma did. She even tried talking to Vivek for me, but he dismissed her concerns just as he'd ignored mine. She and Naina have both emailed me begging me to come back. Even Hema, who supported this plan all along, said it's time to return."

"Who's Hema?"

"She's like an adopted sister. Her parents and mine were close friends. When they died, we took her in. She was actually arranged to be married to Arjun, but he fell in love with Rani and bailed."

"So running away from an arranged marriage is a family tradition, then?"

She laughed. "I guess it is."

They finally pulled up to a building with a large fountain in front and an enormous rotating record on the roof. Divya turned to Ethan, wide-eyed. "What did you do?"

"I called in a favor and bought some studio time so you can cut a demo."

"Ethan!"

"You have a résumé for your career, don't you? Artists have portfolios. If you decide not to do anything with what you produce, consider it a souvenir of our time together." Once again, her heart skipped. Why did she get the feeling he was preparing to say goodbye to her? Had he really fallen in love with her or was this like his love for Pooja? Now that things were getting real, was he getting ready to bolt? Was it all about the chase for him?

He hadn't just bought studio time, he'd also hired

one of the best producers in the field, several technicians and background musicians. Ethan had booked her for twelve hours, which seemed ridiculous for recording the two songs she had written. But when they started, she better understood what it really took. It wasn't just about singing her songs; it was mixing in the music, fine-tuning how background music would be used against her vocals, even touching up her lyrics. The team Ethan had hired were professionals, and they worked hard without a break. Ethan went on food and coffee runs and watched her patiently the whole day. She should've been exhausted at the end of the session, but she was on top of the world. The finished masters were her songs, but they now sounded polished and sophisticated. Her voice had been amplified in the right places and the background music added the depth and symphony her guitar alone couldn't.

"You're like no woman I've ever met. And you can be like no other artist that's out there. You don't have to be like Tina Roy. You don't even have to tour if you don't want to. This right here—" he waved at the studio and the musicians packing up "—this is what making music is all about." He handed her a card and it took her several minutes to recognize it as the one that the man at Café Underground had given them. "The record label is small, but it's legitimate. I had them checked out." He pressed the card into her hand.

She hugged him, unable to find the words to say thank-you. How did he know what she needed when she herself didn't? How was she possibly falling even further in love with him?

They spent the night at his condo. Her family was camped at Arjun's hotel. Vegas was a quick flight, and they would leave in the morning. Ethan offered to take her out to dinner, but she wanted room service. They ordered hamburgers with fries and milkshakes and demolished their plates. She took a shower and wrapped herself in a hotel robe. When she emerged from the bathroom, Ethan whistled.

"Now, this is exactly how I want to see you dressed." He stood and kissed her, then untied the flimsy belt holding the robe together. He slipped his arms around her waist, and she savored the feel of his warm hands across her cool, damp back as he kissed the sensitive spot between her neck and shoulder. He moved his right hand down her back and across her stomach, then reached to touch her between the legs. "You're already wet."

Oh yes I am. "I started without you," she whispered into his ear, kissing him just underneath the earlobe, knowing it drove him crazy. "I want you inside me now." Even through his jeans, she could feel how hard he was.

"Divya," he murmured, moving his hands to her back. She unbuttoned his jeans and pushed them down along with his boxers. He took off his shirt. She pushed him toward the bed then slipped off her robe and straddled him. She rubbed her sensitive nub against him and he moaned, but she didn't hear it. Her slickness against his hardness was driving her mad. Her heart thundered in her chest and her body quivered, desperate for him.

She adjusted her position so he could sheath himself. Then she reached between her legs and pushed him inside her with a roughness that surprised them both. He tensed and stopped, his eyes checking with her to make sure she was okay. Even in the height of passion, he wanted to make sure he wasn't hurting her. Her heart burst inside her chest. For this night with him, she didn't want a parachute. She wanted to free fall for as long as they could. She moved on top of him, up and down, up and down, until she couldn't take it anymore and exploded, screaming his name as she did. She collapsed on top of him, totally spent physically and emotionally.

"Ethan…"

He put his finger on her lips, slipped an arm underneath her and pulled her close. The feel of his breath made her exhale whatever she had pent up inside her.

She'd needed the release to prepare for what was coming tomorrow.

"Ethan, meeting my parents is not like it was for me to come to your house. It'll change my life forever. It'll change my family. It will irreparably fracture the relationship I have with them. If we do this tomorrow, there's no turning back. You understand that, right?"

She couldn't remember his reply because she was so exhausted and comfortable that she fell asleep listening to the beat of his heart.

When she woke the next morning, he was gone.

Sixteen

He nearly dropped the breakfast tray he was carrying when he walked into the bedroom and saw Divya sitting on the bed with her knees pulled into her chest and her head down. She looked up when she heard him, her face streaked with tears. He set the tray on the bed and went to her. She wrapped her arms around him hard, nearly choking him.

"What's going on?"

She shook her head. "Nothing."

"Did you think I left?" The way she tightened her hold told him she had. He pulled her naked body onto his lap, trying to suppress his instant reaction. He rubbed her back. "How could you think I'd leave you like that?"

She kept her face buried in his shoulder, but he

pushed her back so he could look at her. "You think I'll run away, like I did from Pooja?" She didn't answer, but the fear in her eyes told him that was exactly what she was thinking. He cupped her face. "We're going to meet your parents, and I'm going to convince them that I'm the best catch they can ever hope to get for their wayward daughter, and if they don't agree, I'm going to grab your hand like I did at your wedding and fly you away to a place where they'll never find you."

She cracked a smile. "You're not really going to do that."

He lifted his brows. "There's nothing I wouldn't do for you, Divya. I don't have any doubts. I'm not afraid. I love you and I'm going to be there for you."

They ate breakfast and dressed quickly. Divya wore black pants and a blue silk blouse. Her hair was styled and her face painted with almost as much makeup as the day they'd first met. She looked stunningly beautiful but not at all like his Divya.

It was early in the morning, but it took them nearly two hours to get to the airport in rush hour traffic. Once they were seated on the plane, Divya texted him a number.

"What's this?"

"It's my father's number. You're going to call him and tell him that you're bringing me back."

"Like you're a runaway teen?"

"Like you're the hero who finally talked some sense into his rebellious daughter."

"I don't need to lie to your parents to win their approval."

"Oh yes, you do. Things with my family have to be done the proper way. Right now, you are the asshole who crashed the wrong wedding and fled with the bride. My family will say that you're the kind of man who changes women like he changes clothes."

His stomach turned at the way she said this.

"Step one is to reverse your bad image. Our story is that you were helping me get away from what you thought was a forced marriage, because I lied to you. Once you understood that I just wanted to run away, you felt duty bound to return me."

"Have you considered writing screenplays for Bollywood movies?"

"Shut up. We don't have a lot of time to get our story right." She took a sip of the coffee she'd ordered from the flight attendant. "My family will thank you profusely and expect you to be on your way. Next, you're going to say that you have business in Vegas and ask my brother for a hotel recommendation."

"Doesn't he own the Vegas hotel?"

She slapped her hand on her forehead. "Of course he does. That's why he's going to feel obliged to offer you a room. He has an apartment there, where he stays and where my parents and siblings are also staying. This will give you an excuse to stay close to me, and their Indian hospitality will require them to offer to take care of you while you're in Vegas, as a thank-you for returning me safe and sound."

"But I haven't returned you safe and sound. I'm pretty sure I've marked my territory." He wiggled his eyebrows and reached for her, but she slapped him away.

"Pay attention. You're going to spend time with my family and get them to like you. Then I'm going to tell them that I've fallen in love with you. They are going to freak out and try to convince me that you are totally unsuitable. They will spend all their time trying to prove that you are a player, and they'll bring up the whole Pooja situation. It'll get ugly. Under no circumstances will you be rude to them. If you are, there's no turning back."

"Yes, ma'am!" He gave her a mock salute. "So how do I convince them I'm not just some ass taking advantage of their daughter?"

"You are going to go and buy the biggest, most outrageous engagement ring you can find in Vegas." She put the black American Express card he'd given her on the table. "Use this if you have to," she winked at him. "Money should be no object."

"I get it. This is a con, isn't it? You've been with me to get me to buy you an expensive ring that you'll hawk later. I bet your family isn't even rich. I bet they're drowning in debt, and you're going to sell the ring and save the family business."

"Ethan!" She was trying to give him the stern look again, but he noticed her lips twitching. He had absolutely no doubt in his mind that even if he followed her plan to a T, it was all going to go to hell.

"Are you really ready to get married?" He tried to keep his voice light. He wasn't sure which part of her plan was real versus a joke.

"It's not a serious proposal! In my family, showing up with an engagement ring is like asking permission to date me. You need to show my parents that I'm not just some hot piece of ass that you're after. The ring shows how serious you are."

"And this is the part where they'll tell me that I'm not worthy of their daughter and to go back to the trailer park I came from."

She shook her head. "My parents would not know the trailer-park reference."

It was his turn to roll his eyes. "I've seen this movie, Divya, and it's not going to end well. This is where the parents drug the daughter and fly her back to India, where they lock her in the house and marry her off to a bald guy who is twenty years older than her."

Divya laughed. "First of all, I'm quite a catch. My parents would not have to stoop to getting a guy twenty years older than me. Second, if my parents tried doing that, my brothers and sisters would make sure I escaped and reunited with you. Bollywood romances always have a happy ending."

"Do they also have hot sex in the heroine's brother's hotel?" he asked hopefully.

She crossed her arms. "No sex anywhere near my parents. They find out we've been sleeping together and they'll lose all respect for you and me."

He reached out and touched her hand. "We need to play this straight, Divya, tell them outright how we feel about each other and convince them of our love."

She shook her head. "In my family, you don't date unless there's a prospect of marriage. At least, the women don't. The boys are allowed to do whatever the hell they want." The bitterness in her voice was palpable. "But one problem at a time. I don't want them to see our relationship as frivolous. I need them to respect you and understand that we are both serious about continuing our relationship."

"Are they really going to be okay with you being with me?"

"I'll tell them I'm doing it anyway. But this is where you're going to make sure that you charm and disarm them. That's the key to this whole thing."

"And how do you propose I do that? Do you have a ten-point plan for that? Maybe some tips from a Bollywood film?"

She shook her head. "Be yourself. I fell in love with you. They will too."

She pointed to his phone. He took a breath and dialed the number she'd texted him. "It's going to voice mail."

She cursed under her breath. "Hang up."

She held out her hand and he gave her the phone. She punched in another number. "That's my brother Arjun."

This time someone answered, and Ethan recognized the distinct voice of Brother Number One from the wedding. "Mr. Singh? This is Ethan Connors." There was silence on the line. "As you know, your sister and I have been traveling together."

"Where is she?" The voice on the other end was so quietly cold that Ethan shivered.

"She's on my jet and we're inbound to Las Vegas. I'll bring her directly to the Mahal Hotel. I expect we will be there in about one hour." Arjun was silent.

"Look, Mr. Singh, as you know, me crashing the wedding was a big misunderstanding. I was under the mistaken impression that Divya was being forced into the marriage and just wanted to help her. Now that I realize she has to work out her family issues, I'm bringing her back, safe and sound."

Divya raised her thumbs.

Silence on the phone. "You're an idiot. We'll be waiting for you in the lobby." Arjun hung up.

"Well, that went well." He told Divya what Arjun had said and she frowned.

"Maybe we should've left a voice mail for my father. Arjun is a tough nut to crack."

Ethan shook his head. She wasn't going to understand, no matter how he explained it to her. They had to face the firing squad and see if there was anyone left standing when the shooting stopped.

The Tesla was waiting for them when they arrived at the airport. He loaded their suitcases and got to the hotel in record time. His pulse quickened as they pulled into the driveway of the Mahal Hotel. He handed his key card to the valet and resisted the urge to tell him to keep the car close.

Ethan thought he was prepared for what greeted them when they arrived, but he was so wrong. Where normal hotel lobbies bustled with people, this one was empty. Divya's entire family stood in the center of the entrance, in what could only be described as a scene from a mobster movie. Brother One, whom he now knew as Arjun, stood front and center. An older version of Arjun stood beside him with his arms crossed.

A woman who looked remarkably like an older version of Divya narrowed her eyes at him. Brother Two, who he assumed was Sameer, stepped from behind Arjun. Behind them stood ten Men in Black–type guys with their hands on their hips as if they were just waiting for the mob boss to give the signal and they'd pepper the place with bullets.

"Divya!" her mother cried and came rushing toward her. She enveloped Divya in a hug and held on to her while letting out a stream of Hindi that Ethan didn't need a translator to understand. He stepped forward and held out his hand. Arjun took it first and, to his credit, didn't try to squeeze the living daylights out of it, even though his eyes shot daggers at Ethan.

Divya's father was next. "Thank you for bringing her back," he managed with practiced politeness.

Sameer kept his arms crossed, so Ethan retracted his outstretched hand.

"I know we have so much to talk about," Divya gushed. "I'm sorry I upset you all, but I need you to know that Ethan was just trying to help."

"I'm sure he was," Sameer muttered.

Divya powered on. "Ethan, I can't thank you enough. What are your plans?"

Oh boy, that doesn't sound like a practiced question at all. He tried to appear nonchalant. "I have some business in Vegas so I'll be staying a few days."

"Where are you staying?" Divya asked.

"I'll ask my assistant to book me into a hotel."

Silence.

Divya looked pointedly at Arjun. "I can make some

recommendations," he said. Ethan suppressed the urge to laugh, not at all surprised at Arjun's response. He was seeing right through Divya's charade.

"*Bhaiya*, Ethan was very generous in lending me money to buy necessities and the like. Surely we should show him some hospitality."

"How much do we owe you?" Arjun asked coldly.

Ethan shook his head. "It's no trouble at all. Divya and I have become friends. I was happy to help."

Divya glared at him.

Sameer stepped up and whispered something to Arjun. Ethan got the distinct impression it was the Hindi version of "keep your friends close but your enemies closer."

"Why don't you stay here a night while we sort it all out." There was absolutely no warmth or welcome in Arjun's voice.

"Thank you," Ethan muttered.

"My staff will show you to a room. Come on, Divya. We have some catching up to do."

And just like that, her family whisked her away and Ethan was left in the lobby, holding both of their suitcases. He had a sinking feeling that the luggage was all he'd get to keep of Divya.

Seventeen

"Chai for everyone," her mom ordered as soon as they entered Arjun's apartment. It had a beautiful two-story great room in the center and a second-story balcony that wrapped around the space. Rani had designed the apartment, and it felt exactly like their home in Rajasthan. When Divya's parents weren't here, it was serene and private. But her parents came with her mother's attendants, who bustled about making sure everyone was constantly fed, whether they were hungry or not.

Rani came down the stairs holding eight-month-old Simmi. Her sister-in-law looked more beautiful than ever. Motherhood agreed with her. Her hair was held up with a clip in a messy ponytail and she wore a shirt with spit-up on the shoulder. Divya automatically held out her hands for her niece, and Simmi gave a little cackle and came to her. She hugged the baby tightly to her chest, enjoying the feel of the warm, squishy body and the smell of milk and diaper cream. They'd spent a lot of time together in the last several weeks while her wedding was being planned. One advantage of dating America-based Vivek was that Divya had gotten a chance to get to know her sister-in-law and niece. For a second, she wondered what her and Ethan's baby would look like. Would he or she have his beautiful blue eyes?

Karishma and Naina raced down the stairs and enveloped Divya in a hug so tight that the baby protested.

Arjun plucked Simmi from her arms. "You, young lady, have a lot of explaining to do." He pointed to the center of the room where two grand couches and chairs were set up in a square. No matter where she sat, she'd be in the hot seat.

She straightened her back and chose the couch. As predicted, her parents and Arjun sat across from her so she was sitting alone. All eyes were on her. Then Karishma and Sameer plopped down beside her, and she took each of their hands and squeezed gratefully.

One of her mother's maids came around with a tray that held tea served in cups with saucers, along with snacks. Divya refused the tea, craving coffee.

She'd thought a lot about how she was going to approach this meeting, but her mouth was completely dry, and her heart thundered so loudly in her ears that she couldn't hear herself think. She closed her eyes and thought about Ethan, about him holding on to her as they jumped off the plane.

She pulled out the phone Ethan had given her, scrolled to the audio file she needed and played the recording she'd made in LA.

"What's this nonsense?" her mother exclaimed.

"This is my music. Songs I wrote and recorded."

"It's really good," Sameer chimed in. "Who knew you had this kind of talent, sis. You should audition for *American Idol, yaar.*"

"Oh yeah, or that new Indian reality show about rich kids who give up their parents' wealth to pursue their dreams," Naina hollered, clapping her hands.

"Shut up." Arjun glared at Sameer and Naina. "This is why you ran away?"

Divya waved the phone. "I left to explore a dream you would never support. Now I know this is what I want to do with my life. I want to work on my music, be a singer. I never wanted to marry Vivek, and if you guys had listened when I tried to tell you before, I wouldn't have had to run away."

Silence settled over the room, broken only by Simmi's fussing. Rani took the baby and went upstairs, sending a sympathetic look at Divya.

"What is wrong with you, Divya? You are going to throw your life away to become a cheap bar girl?" Her mother's voice was full of fury.

"Being a musician is not like being a bar girl. Look at Lata Mangeshkar."

"Girls from our family don't engage in such professions. You don't want to marry Vivek, fine. We'll find you another boy to your liking," her father said. "Is this the reason you shamed us all by running away from the wedding *mandap*? Do you know all the horrible news stories that circulated about you?"

"I don't want to get married," she yelled, then took a breath. "I want to be independent. I want to make my own decisions, about who I marry, about what I do. I love all of you, but I feel smothered. I can't breathe. I had to run away because none of you would listen to me when I tried to tell you I didn't want to marry Vivek. You forced me into a choice I did not want to make. Now I am telling you what I want, what I need."

"And do your new needs include that *gora*?" her mother asked, her voice dripping with disdain.

No, no, no, this is not the time to talk about Ethan. She didn't want the focus to be on their relationship right now. She wanted to establish her independence with her parents and let them get to know Ethan before bringing him into the picture.

"Divya, it's best to tell them the truth." Divya looked at Arjun. He'd had a similar conversation with his parents when he'd fallen in love with Rani, and she knew he'd struggled with choosing between his family and the love of his life. He nodded encouragingly.

She took a breath. "Yes, Ethan and I are in love and I'm going to keep dating him."

Clank! Her mother set her teacup down with extreme force on the coffee table, cracking the saucer. "This girl has gone mad. Mad, I tell you! You have known that boy for, what, five, six days, and you think you are in love with him?"

Divya looked to Arjun. "How long did it take you to realize you were in love with Rani?"

Arjun looked toward his parents and then at Divya. She silently pleaded with him to help. He'd always been her ally with her parents.

"Americans are not like us, Divya. An Indian boy understands that when he dates a respectable girl, it's with an eye toward marriage. American men date for sex. You will not cheapen yourself like that," her mother said matter-of-factly.

She wanted to tell her parents that their views of Indian men were antiquated, and the realities of modern Indian dating were that men and women pretended chastity in front of their parents and enjoyed themselves behind closed doors.

"How about we invite the dude to dinner and find out what he's thinking? We all know Divya's a little…" Sameer circled his finger near his head and whistled. "Maybe he finds her just as annoying as we do."

Divya gave Sameer a grateful smile. Ethan would follow the plan she'd laid out and show her parents that he was serious and respectable.

"I don't think we should encourage the boy any more than you already have," her father said coldly.

Divya shot Arjun a desperate look, silently pleading with him. Arjun met her gaze and sighed. "I think we should invite the man to dinner, get a feel for him and sort things out."

Her mother looked like she was going to explode, but Arjun stood and put his hand on her shoulder.

Divya knew that Arjun would talk to their mother and calm her down before dinner.

Divya stood. "I'll go invite Ethan."

"You just got here," her father said quietly. He stood and stepped up to Divya, holding his arms out.

She got up and collapsed into his arms, hugging him tightly. The tears she'd been holding back flowed down her cheeks.

"Please, don't leave again, *beti*. Each day you were gone felt like years to me. Like I was missing a piece of my heart, a chunk of my soul."

Sobs choked through her as she settled onto her father's chest and he held her tight, running his hand over her head, like he used to do when she was a little girl and had fallen on the playground. All of the emotions, the pent-up stress, bubbled over, and she felt unable to hold herself up. Sameer wrapped his arms around her from behind, and Arjun, Karishma and Naina joined in. They all held each other for a long time, crying. Divya soaked in their love. *How did I ever think I could live without them?*

When they finally untangled, Divya looked at her mother, who was still seated, drinking her chai. "You must be tired, Divya. Go rest. We will talk tonight at dinner." The firm set of her mother's jaw told her that the night wasn't going to be easy.

"I'm going to go talk to Ethan and let him know about the plans for dinner."

"No need. Arjun will call him and personally invite him. Your sisters have been crying themselves to sleep, missing you. You can wait a few hours to see your *aashiq*." Her mother almost spat out the Hindi word for lover.

"But Ma…"

Her mother held up her hand and cut her eyes to Karishma, who gently took Divya's arm and led her upstairs. Divya's feet moved of their own volition, her eyes glued to the look of anger and disappointment on her mother's face.

They went to the room she'd be sharing with Karishma, who talked nonstop and insisted on getting all the details. *Five hundred rooms in this hotel and we all have to stay in the same apartment.* But there was an advantage to sharing with Karishma: she could sneak off to go spend the night with Ethan and Karishma would cover for her.

Naina and Sameer joined them, and her siblings filled her in on everything that had happened immediately following her wedding escape.

"I swear, Divya, I thought Dad would have a heart attack when Arjun and Sameer returned without you after you ran out of the hotel gardens," Naina said. Divya's stomach soured. "But that was nothing compared to what happened after the social media posts started and they found out who Ethan was. I love that BrideSnatcher hashtag."

Sameer chimed in. "There were all kinds of conspiracy theories. Somehow the Indian media latched on to the idea that you and Ethan were planning a secret takeover of our family business to overthrow Arjun."

Divya gasped. Such a thing was unfathomable, but

she could see how the media could get out of control. Family feuds were the bedrock of Bollywood movies.

"Arjun and Dad had to fly overnight to India to calm the shareholders," Sameer said, his voice suddenly quiet.

Divya's head hurt. How could she have been so irresponsible? If she'd stopped to think about her actions, she would've seen all this happening. Arjun hadn't gone to India for Karishma's college graduation because he didn't want to leave Simmi, yet he'd had to leave his wife and baby because of her. Her chest was uncomfortably tight. She barely heard everything else her siblings had to say.

"I should check my email," Divya said weakly.

Sameer nodded. "That would be good. We've had some problems with the contracts for the new hotel in Washington. I could use your help."

Knowing that she had a lot to catch up on, her siblings left as soon as she opened her laptop. She turned on her regular phone, which Karishma had thoughtfully plugged in. There was no way she could possibly get through all of the text messages, but she sent replies to Hema and her close friends, letting them know that she was okay and promising to talk to them soon.

As she immersed herself in her work email, she didn't notice the buzzing of the phone Ethan had given her. She'd discovered that Sameer had downplayed the disaster he and Arjun had to deal with. Investors were threatening to pull out of their new project in DC, and several urgent contracts that she had prepared before the wedding remained unsigned. Sameer had been worried about her and hadn't been able to focus on the work. She'd seen this pattern before: first his work suffered, then the pressure of catching up got to him. If she didn't take over now, he would spiral, and once that happened, recovery took months. She had to stop it before it got worse.

I've only been thinking about myself.

Karishma reappeared, holding a tray of tea and snacks. "We'd better start getting ready for dinner."

Divya gasped as she realized that hours had gone by. She guiltily grabbed Ethan's phone to see several missed messages from him. "I need to go see him," she said to Karishma.

"Div, dinner is only an hour away. You can wait that long, can't you? Or are you all hot for him?" She hugged herself and made kissy faces.

"Stop! I need to talk to him before he comes over here. Cover for me." With that, she stepped outside to the balcony and looked down at the great room to make sure the coast was clear. Ethan had texted her his room number and she went straight down. Arjun had given him one of the best suites in the hotel.

As soon as she arrived, Ethan pulled her into his arms and held her tight. "I was afraid you'd forgotten about me already."

Tears stung her eyes. "We need to talk."

Eighteen

Ethan didn't need her to spell it out for him. He saw it all over her face. She'd been sucked back into the family fold.

"I love you." It's all he had left to say to her.

She sniffed. "And I love you. Change of plans."

"We're switching from a Bollywood plot to a Hollywood one?"

She rolled her eyes but couldn't help smiling. "I need to prep you for dinner with my parents. They know we're involved. They are going to grill you about—"

He kissed her. "Divya, I got this."

She stared at him. "You don't understand. Things have to be…"

He looked into her deep dark eyes, trying to tell her without words that he'd do anything for her, that he finally understood what it meant to love someone. She had shown him how real relationships worked. She'd brought him closer to his family; now it was time for him to do the same for her.

She looked at him uncertainly. He cupped her face, then bent his head and pressed his lips softly to hers. "I'm ready."

One thing was clear: if Divya was going to be happy with him, her family had to accept him.

Divya put on a conservative black dress, did her makeup and added the right amount of jewelry. When she went downstairs, it was clear that her mother approved. She was the last one to arrive. Everyone was dressed somewhat formally. Even Simmi was wearing a cute red dress and had a little bow in the few wisps of hair on her head.

Divya's stomach churned. She'd forgotten to tell Ethan to dress up. His standard-issue jeans and polo would not go over well. She rubbed her temples. *This is going to be a disaster.*

The table was set for dinner, and waiters stood in the corner ready with a tray of *samosas* and *pakoras*. She looked at the time and cringed. Ethan was a minute late.

The bell rang and she rushed to answer it, but one of the staff beat her to it. Her heart stopped when she saw him. He was wearing a perfectly fitted black suit with a French-cuffed shirt. *Wow.* Even though she'd just seen him a half hour ago, she needed to touch him. To make sure he knew that she loved him.

Arjun stepped forward to greet Ethan, and her heart swelled at the sight of her brother shaking Ethan's hand and slapping him on the arm. Her parents were standing by the living room couches, and Arjun escorted Ethan to them. "I don't think we formally introduced everyone," Arjun said good-naturedly. Divya guessed that Rani had talked to Arjun, perhaps reminded him how difficult it was for them when they first announced their love.

Ethan stepped to her parents and bent down and touched their feet. Divya gasped. She hadn't briefed him on *pairi pauna,* an Indian tradition where you touched the feet of your elders as a show of respect and to get their blessings. She'd never expected Ethan to understand an archaic custom like that, nor had she felt comfortable asking him to do it. Rani had told her all about the first time she'd met Divya's parents. Arjun had asked her to do *pairi pauna* and Rani had felt disrespected. Being Indian, she didn't agree with the custom. Divya never expected Ethan to understand.

She leaned against the wall to steady herself, her knees suddenly weak. A hushed silence fell in the room. Her mother's hand instinctively touched Ethan's head in blessing, just like it would when Arjun or Sameer touched their feet. Divya could almost see her mother's heart melting.

"What would you like to drink, Ethan?" Sameer broke the stunned silence.

"A beer would be great." Divya did a mental face palm. She'd forgotten to tell him about the family drink.

"I'm sure room service has some," Sameer said easily.

"Whatever you're having is fine," Ethan amended.

Sameer handed Ethan a tumbler of whiskey. Ethan gallantly took a sip and tried not to grimace as he swallowed. Divya noticed Sameer also had a tumbler in his hand and she frowned. He wasn't supposed to be drinking. While he was addicted to painkillers, his therapist had warned her that any substance use could cause a relapse.

The waiters circulated with the appetizers, but no one seemed hungry.

"He's really hot, especially in a suit. I hope you've seen him without all those clothes?" Karishma whispered. Divya shushed her before their mother's owl ears caught wind of their conversation. Her parents still thought she was a virgin. It had always galled her that they never had that expectation of her brothers, but now was not the time to dwell on the gender hypocrisy in her family.

"Tell us, Ethan, how is it that five days ago, you professed your love in front of all of us, thinking Divya was another woman, and now you're here to convince us that we should trust our daughter to you?" Apparently her mother wasn't going to give Ethan a chance to settle in.

Divya silently pleaded with Ethan to go with the story she'd concocted: that Pooja was his best friend and had asked him to save her from the wedding. Ethan was facing enough judgment just being American.

"There's this notion of love at first sight. It seems

irrational to believe in something like that. It feels like it only happens in films. I was indeed trying to break up my ex-girlfriend's wedding, but that's because I'd talked myself into wanting to love her. I'd lost hope that I'd find the kind of love I was looking for. And then I met Divya."

Divya sighed. She knew Ethan meant well. He was trying to be genuine, but he had no idea what he'd just done.

"Wah! Karan Johar couldn't have written a better line." The sarcastic comment came from Divya's father. Ethan had no idea who Karan Johar was, but now was not the time to ask.

Divya had warned him to expect her parents to be blunt, and they clearly weren't wasting time. Not even a minute or two of polite small talk? He didn't want to play the games Divya had suggested. He wanted to be honest with her parents. If he and Divya were going to have a future together, he needed to develop a relationship with her parents too. He'd spent his entire life feeling like an outsider in his family; he would not be the man who created a rift with hers. He would win them over. He had to.

"How do you know this time it's real, and you're not mistaken again?"

"Dad," Divya said pleadingly.

"Why don't we sit down to dinner?" The soothing compromise was offered by Rani, who was struggling to hold on to her wiggly baby while carrying a bowl of baby food.

Divya took the baby from Rani's arms, expertly turned Simmi around and settled her on her hip, giving her a kiss on the head, all in one move. The baby giggled and extended her pudgy little hands to touch Divya's face. Ethan's chest constricted. Everything he ever wanted was right there next to him. He just had to be strong enough to get it.

Rani took the baby back from Divya and settled her into a high chair. She waved for everyone to take their seats. Divya motioned to Ethan, who took a seat next to her and grabbed her hand under the table. She quickly pulled it out of his grip. All eyes were on them.

"If the whiskey isn't to your liking, we can order some beer," Arjun said, nodding towards the still-full tumbler Ethan had set down on the table.

"It's great," Ethan responded and lifted the glass to his lips, his stomach curling at the smell of the whiskey. He could almost see his dad sitting at the dining room table, glass in hand, barely looking at him as he signed the papers disowning him. His own father hadn't wanted him. How did he expect Divya's family to accept him?

Six waiters appeared, each carrying a different dish. They went from person to person, ladling food onto their plates. Ethan swallowed the bitter-tasting whiskey.

"So, tell me, Ethan. Why do you want to date a girl from India? Surely there are plenty of American women who'd be interested in you. Someone you have more in common with." Divya's dad's tone was friendly but his eyes stared Ethan down.

Ethan took a breath. "Divya and I have a connection, we understand each other. Where we're from doesn't matter as much as how we feel about each other."

"That is a very naive view of the world. Do you think it won't matter that you two come from very different worlds, that your culture, your traditions are nothing alike?" Rani's mother could freeze lava with the ice in her voice.

"Culture and tradition don't define who we are. Our values do. I was also raised in a very close-knit family. No matter where I am in the world, I always go home for all family birthdays and special events. My parents have an incredible relationship, and that's what I want."

"How long did your parents date before they got married?" Divya's father was not cutting him any slack, but Ethan was no slouch. He hadn't built his company into a billion-dollar empire by being a pushover. But the stakes had never been this high.

"How long did you and Mrs. Singh date before you were married?" He knew the answer to that question, which is why he asked. Divya's parents had an arranged marriage. They had never gotten the chance to date, but from what she'd told him, her parents genuinely loved each other and had built a successful life together.

Divya's mother didn't miss a beat. "Our marriage was based on a firm grounding of shared values and expectations. Our families knew each other. We were raised with the same traditions, wanted the same things out of life, understood how our lives would work." She took a breath. "Tell me, in which country will you live? Where will you raise your children?"

"Ma, we're only dating. We haven't even talked about marriage. These details aren't that important right now," Divya said, exasperated.

"No, Divya, these are the decisions that tear families apart. This is exactly why we prescreen boys for you. We have generations of experience in these matters, but you kids only think about today. Now you are dating, tomorrow you will want to get married and then you'll have children. Will your children be raised Hindu or Christian?"

"We will teach them both of our religions," Divya said.

"I'm agnostic," Ethan answered at the same time.

"You see. These are not trivial things," her mom said smugly.

"Ethan, why don't you tell us a little more about your family," Arjun said diplomatically, and Ethan released a breath, glad to be on to a safe topic.

When he was done with describing his family, Divya's siblings asked him impersonal questions about his business, clearly trying to ease the tension around the dinner table. At some point, Sameer and Karishma deftly moved the conversation to easy topics like movies and politics. Without thinking, they slipped between English and Hindi as they spoke, Divya included. When they weren't grilling him, the family had an easy way with each other, and he had to keep himself from staring at the beautiful smile on Divya's face when she looked affectionately around the table.

At one point, Naina asked him a question, and he had no idea she was speaking to him. Divya elbowed him. "I'm sorry, I didn't catch that."

Naina smacked her head. "Sorry, Ethan, we don't even realize when we're speaking Hinglish."

He smiled gamely. He was used to being the odd man out, the one who didn't fit in. He took another bite of chicken. It burned his throat, and the whiskey soured his stomach.

"You haven't eaten much, Ethan. The food not to your liking?" Divya's mother asked.

He knew it was irrational, but he could swear she could read his mind. "The food is great. I'm just enjoying the conversation."

She scoffed. "A conversation you only half understand, just like this family. You've only seen one side of Divya."

Anger surged through him. It was one thing to question his motives but another to insult him. He turned to Divya, expecting her to stand up for him, to say something to her parents, but she resolutely avoided meeting his gaze. A familiar ache settled into his chest. Divya didn't know it right now, but she was going to reject him, just like all the other women in his life.

Nineteen

"Let's have dessert in the kitchen," Rani suggested.
Divya shot her sister-in-law a grateful look. It hadn't
been easy for Rani to fit into the family, but she'd
found a way to take control of her house. It would eventually be okay with Ethan too. *Wouldn't it?*

The kitchen island was far more informal than the
dining room table and it would help Ethan relax. She'd
felt the tension in his muscles all through dinner. She'd
tried to warn him about how difficult her parents could
be, had told him how to handle things. But he was ig-
noring her advice. Did he want to sabotage this dinner?

It was a large island with several counter chairs.
Rani excused herself to put the baby to sleep. The staff
served chai, coffee and *kheer*, an Indian rice pudding
that Ethan seemed to enjoy. Divya made a point to keep

the conversation in English. She hadn't realized just how much they spoke in Hindi. Sameer made a gallant effort to keep the conversation on neutral topics. It felt stilted, as it had at dinner. Divya thought about Gauri's comments about her American sister-in-law. Would it always be awkward to have Ethan around her family?

After dinner, Arjun directed Divya and Ethan to the study for a nightcap. From the look on Ethan's face, he would rather have drunk more whiskey. The study was cozy with book-lined shelves, a couch and two leather chairs around a coffee table.

Ethan and Divya were left alone. She didn't need to hear what was going on outside the study to know that her siblings were being dismissed and her parents were plotting.

Ethan reached for her hand, but she eyed the door. "While I'd like nothing more than to throw you down on that couch and kiss you senseless, I know PDA is not okay. I just want to touch you for a second."

She smiled and took his outstretched hand. He pulled her closer to him.

"You're doing great," she said.

He smiled. "You're a really bad liar."

She looked into his impossibly blue eyes. "You can do this."

"And what if I can't?"

"You have to." She'd meant it as a joke, but her voice held a high, desperate note. He placed his forehead on hers and she leaned into him.

"Divya!" Her father's shout as he and her mother

entered the room made Divya jump away from Ethan like he was radioactive.

She took a seat in the leather chair, forcing Ethan to take the other chair. He couldn't resist touching her, and her mother's eagle eyes wouldn't miss how physically comfortable they were with each other.

"So, Ethan, what do you know about Divya's new singing career?" Her mother could teach a class in making a loaded question sound friendly.

Ethan exhaled while she tensed. He had no idea what was coming. "I think she's incredibly talented."

"Do you think it's a respectable profession?"

Ethan frowned. "I think it's a legitimate career, just like being in business. Entertainers in this country are highly valued."

"So you'd be okay with Divya wearing skimpy clothes and dancing around a stage while drunk men ogle her."

Ethan took a sharp breath. "That's a stereotype of entertainers that doesn't have to be true. Divya can do what she's comfortable with, and I'll support her."

"So you're the one who's been encouraging Divya to pursue this crazy plan to give up her law career and become a singer," her father said accusingly.

"He helped me understand what I wanted. He generously bought studio time so I could explore my musical abilities," Divya interjected.

Ethan turned to her parents. "Divya has an amazing talent and deserves our support to pursue a new career."

"Singing is a hobby. Divya, if you really want to

pursue this, we can buy you all the studio time you want." Her mother leaned forward. "You had your fun. It's time to come back to real life."

Divya bristled. Her parents didn't get to decide what she wanted for her *real life*. "This is something I have to do for myself, Ma. I want to live my life on my terms. The way I want."

"Just a few days with this American and you've forgotten your whole upbringing," her mother muttered.

"Mrs. Singh, I respect your culture and your point of view, but Divya is an intelligent, independent woman. She has the right to make her own decisions, to choose what she wants to do with her career and whom to date."

"And as her parents, we have the responsibility to protect her from bad influences," her father said pointedly. "Look, Ethan, in our family, you don't get to *date* our daughter. We believe in old-fashioned values. You talk about respect. A man who cares about our daughter would show more respect for her family traditions."

Ethan's jaw clenched.

Divya tried to catch his eye, silently telling him that now was the time to pull out the engagement ring she'd asked him to buy and ask her parents for her hand in marriage. After a heavy silence that seemed to weigh them all down, her mother turned to Ethan. "Let us get to the point of this conversation. What is your relationship with our daughter? What are your intentions toward her?"

He straightened and looked both her parents in the eyes. "I love your daughter."

Divya breathed a sigh of relief. She knew that the romantic way to do things was to propose to the girl on bended knee, but that's not how it was done in Indian families. Ethan knew what a big deal it was for her to introduce someone like him to her parents. They needed to see that he wasn't a stereotype, that he held the same values her family did.

"I hope we'll have a future together. With your permission, I'd like to keep seeing her."

Divya glared at him. *What is he doing?*

"Excuse me, Mr. Connors, our daughter is not someone you try out to see if she is to your liking," her mother said icily. "Clearly, you don't understand or respect our family values."

Ethan stood. Every muscle in his body was rigid, his hands clenched tightly at his sides. "Excuse me, Mrs. Singh, Divya is not your property, and she does not need to put up with this. You have no idea what we share, and I will not let you insult her like this."

Divya jumped from her seat and looked from Ethan to her parents and back again. *What are you doing, Ethan?* They had talked about this very scenario, and she'd reminded him that under no circumstances could he be rude to her parents.

Ethan had done everything she'd asked him not to do. It was as if he was purposely sabotaging the whole thing. Then it hit her.

She thought back to something Rajiv had said to her in New York. Now the words haunted her.

It's not that he's American. It's that he doesn't take

relationships seriously. For him this is a game, an amusement.

When he'd gotten to Pooja's wedding, he'd realized that he had been impulsive and didn't really want to marry her. The same thing was happening now. He'd done what he always did when things got real. He'd pulled the safety parachute.

This was the moment when he'd find out whether their love could withstand the ultimate test. He had come with every intention to win over her family, but now he was clear on the fact that he would never win her parents' approval. Not only that, it wasn't the right environment for her. She loved singing; the day they had spent at the studio had energized and exhilarated her. Divya wasn't a corporate lawyer, and if she stayed with her family, they would crush her spirit.

But could she stand up to her family? Could she give them up for him? If she had to choose, would she choose him?

He held out his hand to her. "Come with me, Divya. My plane is ready to take you anywhere you want to go, and I'll be with you. I'll take care of you."

Time stopped. Their eyes locked and he tried to tell her how much he loved her, how badly he wanted her to choose him.

He didn't know if it was a few seconds later or several minutes when Divya slowly shook her head and backed away from him.

"Divya, now's the time to take a stand. Run away with me. Again."

Her eyes shone. "Ethan, I can't." Her voice broke, and along with it, his heart shattered.

She'd made her choice, and it wasn't him.

Twenty

Divya set her bag down and sat wearily on the old couch that she'd gotten at a yard sale. At least the temperature in New York City was much cooler than in Rajasthan.

She looked around the small apartment. Her bathroom at home was bigger than the entire five-hundred-square-foot efficiency, which included a galley kitchen, bathroom and bedroom/living room. The entire closet wasn't even big enough for her shoe collection, but luckily all she'd come with was a suitcase worth of stuff and a Martin guitar.

This was the best she could afford right now, and she was fine with that. Arjun had offered to give her money, but she'd refused. Rajiv and Gauri had invited her to live with them. They were centrally located in

Manhattan, and it would've made her life easier than
commuting into the city more than an hour each way
on buses and the subway. She had a small advance
from the contract she'd signed with East Side Records,
and for now, it was enough to pay the rent on this small
place in New Jersey.

She ran her hand over the guitar. It was her only
connection to Ethan. After he'd walked out on the dinner with her parents, she'd gone knocking on his hotel
room door only to find the room empty. He wouldn't
answer her calls, texts or emails. Why wouldn't he
even give her a chance to explain?

The answer was plain as day. He'd realized he'd
been impulsive again and done what he did best: give
up.

It had been six months since that fateful dinner and
not a day went by when she thought about whether she
should have gone with him. *But how could she have?*
She'd seen Sameer drinking that night at dinner, and
she couldn't leave without making sure he was okay.
Her worst fears had come true when she'd found Sameer in bed the next morning, clearly hungover. She'd
hoped it was just alcohol but knew enough from her
research about addiction to know that he was in trouble. She had returned to India with her parents and siblings, to wallow in self-pity and watch over Sameer.
Her parents assumed that she had come to her senses
regarding Ethan. She'd slipped into her old life like a
familiar pair of jeans that went with everything but
felt a little too tight.

She searched Ethan's name on Google every day,

and while there were articles about his company, he had disappeared from public life. It was as if he'd been a figment of her imagination. Then a month later, the Martin guitar had showed up at her house in India. There was no note, but she knew what he was trying to tell her.

She'd been miserable in her regularly scheduled life. The work of lawyering brought her no joy. Her mother dragging her to social events made her want to scream. Then the guitar had arrived, and she'd realized that just because Ethan was gone didn't mean that she had to go back to her old life. She had fled her wedding in search of her dream. A dream that could turn into reality. It was time to follow through.

She'd sent her demo to East Side Records and they had asked her to come to New York.

Sameer had still been lying to her about his addiction, and she'd finally called Arjun and told him what was going on with their brother. With typical take-charge efficiency, Arjun found the best rehab facility in the United States and flew Sameer there in the family jet. Sameer's continued relapses had finally made her realize that she had done him a disservice by trying to manage his addiction herself.

She'd packed her bags, left her parents a note along with a special item for her mom, and bought an economy class ticket on a commercial plane to New York.

The album with East Side Records was being released next week.

Her phone buzzed with a video call from Sameer. She clicked and greeted her brother. Sameer had stayed in the facility for ninety days and had been out for two months. "How's the next Beyoncé settling into her new space?"

She grinned back at her brother, noting how great he looked. He'd been sober for five months, and she had nothing to do with it. "It's a little basic, but I don't need much." She turned the camera to show him.

"Basic? Div, our servants live in better quarters than that. I don't understand why you won't use your bank accounts. Ma and Dad haven't cut you off, you know. Stop being stubborn and call them. I'm sure they'll come to the launch party if you personally invite them."

"I sent them the invitation."

He shook his head. "I don't know who's more stubborn, you or them."

"I will not be held hostage emotionally."

Her parents' plan had almost worked. The entire time she'd been back in India, her parents had reminded her of her responsibility and duty to the family. If Ethan hadn't sent the guitar, she would've slipped further into her old life. But leaving India made her realize that she'd faced her worst fear, and she was fine. As Arjun reminded her, he'd been forgiven for wanting to marry Rani, and eventually Divya would be forgiven too. She had to wait out their parents.

"Well, I am not staying in that dump when I come next week, but I do have a surprise for you that should be arriving any second."

As if on cue, someone knocked on the door. She opened it and a deliveryman handed her a giant box from Naeem Khan, one of her favorite designers, known for his Indian-influenced dresses. She squealed and set the phone on the coffee table so Sameer could see her unbox it. "You didn't!"

"My sister is not going to launch her first album wearing something off-the-rack."

Divya pulled out the beautiful gown. It was pale pink with a sheer black layer embellished with intricate embroidery. She excused herself to put it on and it fit perfectly. The asymmetric neckline was striking, and the hem was just the right length for the heels that were included in the box.

"Oh my God, I love it." She twirled in front of the phone's camera for Sameer to see.

"I asked Ma to contact your tailor in India to send your measurements to the New York boutique. I think she's ready to forgive you."

Divya ignored his comment. "This dress is way too tasteful for something you would pick out and way too risqué for Ma's tastes."

"I had help," he said slyly.

She narrowed her eyes. "Sameer, are you already dating? You know what the therapist said about taking time to be by yourself."

He rolled his eyes. "She's just a friend. Relax." Then his voice became serious. "You don't have to worry about me, Div. I'm really good this time." She believed him. He sounded different—stronger, more confident. "Arjun and Rani have been amazing in supporting me, and Karishma's really stepped up with the India office. She's way better than you were."

Divya smiled. She hadn't given her younger sister enough credit for being ready to step up. She'd always see her as the little girl who pulled her pigtails and stole her toys.

"Karishma is so good, she actually got the family jet for her and Naina to come to New York for your launch party."

Divya's heart filled with love for her siblings. They'd banded together to support her, and yet it felt like a piece of her soul was missing.

"Have you invited him?"

Sameer didn't have to say who he meant. They both knew. She shook her head.

"Want me to invite him?"

"Don't you dare. I've tried contacting him. If he wanted to talk to me, he knows how to get hold of me."

"Have you ever thought about the fact that he was right in running away? You didn't exactly stand up for him with Ma and Dad. Even I wasn't sure that you really wanted to be with him. You seemed to be unsure of what you wanted."

"It's what he does, Sam. He decides to take something on full steam ahead and when it gets real, he runs away. It's best I forget about him."

"You don't seem okay," Sameer said.

She pasted a smile on her face. "Of course I am. I'm just jittery getting ready for the record launch." After she hung up the phone, she ran her hands over the guitar. She wasn't okay. Her parachute hadn't opened and she didn't know what to do. She was hurtling toward the ground, and Ethan wasn't there to pull the cord.

Twenty-One

Ethan stared at the phone, unwilling to believe what his mother had just said.

"Divya's mother specifically said Matt, Heather and the kids are included in the invitation to Divya's record launch."

Divya's mother had called his? He rubbed his neck, looking out at the view of the Hudson River from his Upper West Side condo.

"The kids are really excited to go. They've been asking about Divya."

"You can use my plane," he said flatly.

"Hon, there's got to be a way to patch things up," his mother said.

No, there isn't. He had changed his cell phone number and email address, closed all his social media accounts. He didn't want to weaken and answer Divya's call. Yet not an hour went by when he didn't think about her, when he didn't worry about her, when he didn't miss her. He had consoled himself with the knowledge that she'd be happier without him in the long term.

"Mom, you weren't there that night. You should've seen her face when I stood up to her parents. Her heart broke right in front of me. If we stayed together, our love would be a constant battle in her house. It would ruin the amazing relationship she has with her family. She'd feel like a part of her was missing. I don't want that life for her. Marrying an Indian woman means marrying her family."

"Mrs. Singh invited you too."

"Are you sure?"

"I think it's her way of reaching out to you."

He still couldn't believe that Divya's mother had called to invite his family to her launch party. Six months had gone by. He was sure by now they'd have found her another Vivek to marry.

"If you ask me, I think she sounded incredibly sad. We talked for over an hour. She asked me a lot of questions about you and about our family. She sounded really nice."

"That's why I'm wondering if it was really her," Ethan said.

Marilyn chuckled. "You know, Ethan, ever since middle school, I've watched you crush on one girl after another. You always cancel the relationship before it really begins, because you're so afraid the girl will break up with you."

He looked at the picture sitting on his kitchen counter. It was the only personal item in his otherwise sterile condo. A picture of him and Divya and Allie and Jake on a giant teddy bear. It was exactly what he wanted.

He remembered what Divya had told him the first day they met. She wanted to be independent; she didn't want to get saddled down with a husband and children. Now that she was on the way to achieving her dream, he wouldn't be the one to hold her back. She deserved to get everything she wanted in life.

Out of habit, he touched the little box in his pocket. It was the ring he'd bought for Divya when they'd arrived in Vegas on the day he was scheduled to meet her parents. He carried it with him everywhere he went, unable to let it go.

"You should all attend, but I won't be coming," he said to his mother, a note of finality in his voice. "Tell Divya I wish her well."

It was her night. She looked amazing. She stood backstage, waiting for her cue to make a grand entrance. She should feel nervous, excited, maybe even scared, but all she felt was empty. What was the point of this success if she couldn't share it with the people she loved? Maybe she had been too stubborn. She should have called her parents. She should have called Ethan.

"There she is."

Divya turned to see Arjun making his way toward her with Karishma, Naina, Rani and Sameer right behind him. Sameer stretched out his arms to pull her into a hug, but Karishma slapped him away. "Do not ruin her makeup or hair right before she goes onstage. Look how perfect she looks."

"You do clean up nice, sis," Sameer quipped.

It had been four months since she'd left home and seen all her siblings together and her heart swelled. "Did Ma and—?"

"We came."

Divya turned to see her parents step toward her from the shadows.

"How could we miss this?" her father said.

Divya didn't hesitate. She ran into her father's outstretched arms and buried her face in his chest, not caring whether her hair and makeup were ruined. He put his hand on her head. "*Beti,* we are not going to agree with all the decisions you make, but that doesn't mean we don't love you. And it does not give you the right to cut us out of your life."

She turned to her mother, who looked brilliant in a royal blue saree with silver thread woven through it. Diamond solitaires glittered in her ears. She held out her hand and Divya took it, squeezing it tightly.

"Ma, our family means the world to me. But I don't want the life you've chosen for me. It's okay if you don't accept Ethan. We aren't together anyway. But I need you to support me in my career. You have to trust that you raised me right, and I wouldn't do anything to embarrass myself and or my family."

Her mother dabbed at her eyes. "You know, your father went directly to your grandfather and asked to marry me, and my father said yes. I was so angry that he made this decision without asking me that I ran away."

Divya's eyes widened. Her mother was always so proper; she'd never imagined her doing something so rebellious.

"Someone reminded me what it's like to be forced to give up something you love to do." Her mother's voice cracked, and she pointed to her feet. Divya looked down and her mother lifted her saree. She was wearing the *ghunghuru,* the little bells Divya had bought her right before she'd moved to New York.

Tears prickled Divya's eyes. "I never told you this, Ma, but my love of music started when I listened to the sounds of your *ghunghuru.* I used to watch you from the crack in the bedroom door and sing to the sounds of the bells on your feet."

Her mother wiped a tear from her cheek. "I guess I'm to blame for this whole singing thing, then."

Divya smiled. "And also the running-away thing."

"If you guys are all done being sentimental, we should head out to the party and let Divya get ready for her big performance," Sameer said.

They all wished her well. When her mother was out of earshot her father turned to her. "You know, Divya, there was someone I loved before I married your mother."

She looked at her father. It wasn't a secret, but he never talked about it. "Arjun's mother," she whispered.

He nodded. "I know what it's like to fall in love with someone your parents don't approve of, and I know how it can rip your heart into pieces. When Arjun wanted to marry Rani, we stood in his way because I thought she would tear this family apart. Instead, she's helped us see that it isn't the worst thing in the world to have an American son-in-law. The worst thing is losing you. You don't have to give up your music, and you don't have to give up Ethan."

She smiled for her father's benefit. She hadn't given up Ethan. He'd given up on her.

Ethan stood outside the ballroom, listening to the sounds of the party inside, knowing that Divya was just beyond the doors. Allie texted him every few minutes, giving him a play-by-play of what was going on inside. They'd met Divya's parents, whom Allie described as *totally cool*.

He hadn't intended to come. Wasn't even dressed for the occasion. But he hadn't been able to resist. All he wanted was one look at her. A last look.

"Ethan!"

He looked up to see Rani emerge from the ballroom. "What're you doing out here?"

He smiled, but his throat was so tight he couldn't speak. She looked at him kindly, then motioned to the armchairs in the hallway. He took a seat and she sat next to him.

"You know, when Arjun and I first got together, his mother convinced me that our relationship was doomed to fail. I almost didn't marry Arjun because of his parents."

Ethan looked up in surprise. Rani seemed to fit in so well with the family.

"They're not bad people, it just takes a while to open their minds. They're like ice cream when you first take it out of the freezer, cold and hard and unyielding. But give it enough time, and they melt into sweetness."

"Thank you, Rani. But it's not about your in-laws. I don't want to hold her back. She ran away from her wedding because she didn't want to get saddled with marital obligations. She's finally found her freedom and voice. It's time for her to live her dream. I don't fit into her plans."

"But you fit with Divya, and that's all that matters." She put her hand on his. "I'm not saying it all works out, but when you love someone, it's worth the sacrifices."

"I don't want to hold her back."

She looked toward the ballroom doors where the CEO of the record company had just started speaking. "When Divya wants to do something, I've never known her to let anything stop her. Don't you think you're holding her back by making decisions for her?"

He sighed. What was the right answer here?

Rani put her hand on his and he looked up at her. "Do you love her?"

He didn't hesitate. "More than anything."

"Then, tell her."

He smiled. "Would you help me with something?"

Twenty-Two

Divya stood on the stage in her beautiful gown as East Side Records's CEO introduced her. She ran her hands over the wood of her guitar. She didn't need the guitar—there was a quartet of musicians onstage to provide the instrumentation for her song. She needed to feel the wood beneath her fingers, to remember Ethan's faith in her.

The ballroom had been decorated with sarees and lanterns to celebrate her Hinglish songs. Sameer waved from the front of the crowd, and her heart soared as her mother blew her a kiss.

She searched frantically for Ethan. *He has to be here, he has to be here.* She mouthed Ethan's name when she caught Sameer's eye, but he shook his head and her heart sank into her toes. *He really isn't coming.*

When it was time to sing, she stepped up to the microphone. Her stomach churned and her legs felt like wooden posts. A sea of people stared at her. Cameras flashed and bright lights shone down on her. She knew her performance was being broadcast live. It wasn't just the people in the room who'd be watching her.

The musicians started the instrumental introduction to her song. There was no voice in her throat. *I can't do this.*

Then the ballroom door opened and Ethan entered, his eyes focused on her.

Her breath released from her chest. He raised his thumb, and she began to sing the song she'd written for him. She sung her heart out, needing him to feel her voice, to understand that she loved him with every fiber of her being.

People burst into applause and she performed two more songs. She lost track of Ethan in the crowd, but she knew he was there. She could feel his presence and that was all that mattered.

When she was finished, the roar of the crowd was deafening. The CEO was back onstage. It was her cue to leave so he could make his closing speech, but he motioned for her to stay. "Before you leave, Divya, we have a special presentation."

She looked in surprise as her parents and Ethan walked onto the stage. He stood in front of her and looked at her with such longing that her legs threatened to buckle underneath her. He dropped to one knee and a hush fell over the crowd.

"I'm sorry I was such an ass and didn't realize how much you meant to me."

They were the same words he'd said when he'd crashed her wedding.

"Must you always show up in such a dramatic fashion?" Tears stung her eyes, and her heart felt like it would burst if he didn't touch her soon.

"I've been an idiot."

"Yes, you have."

"I don't need a house. I don't need children. All I need is you."

She shook her head. "I need at least three-point-four children, but not now, in a few years."

He pulled out a ring box and opened it. "I bought you the biggest ring I could find in Vegas."

Vegas? He'd bought the ring months ago? Tears streamed down her cheeks. She didn't know whether she wanted to kiss him or punch him.

"I'm a poor musician now. I'm going to sell that ring for cash."

He held his hand out and she placed hers on top of it.

"Will you marry me for my money?"

She shook her head. "I can make my own money."

He stayed on his knee, his eyes so impossibly blue, so full of love that her heart burst in her chest.

"I love you, Divya. You make me a better man, you give me strength and I want to spend the rest of my life becoming the man you deserve. Will you marry me?" He'd said the words in perfect Hindi.

She couldn't speak through the lump in her throat,

so she nodded as hard as she could. He slipped the ring onto her finger.

He stood and she fell into his arms.

"Kiss! Kiss!" the crowd chanted, and he obliged. She drank him in, her knees suddenly unable to hold her up, but she knew she wouldn't fall. He'd hold on to her for the rest of their lives.

Her mother stepped forward and placed a hand on his shoulder. Divya looked at her, silently pleading with her not to ruin the moment. "Ethan, welcome to the family."

Her mother joined her hands together in silent apology. Then Divya was hugging her parents, and before she knew it, her father and her siblings and Matt and Heather and the kids were all onstage, and she and Ethan were in the center of a giant group hug.

"Run away with me?" she asked.

"My jet is waiting."

* * * * *

Make sure not to miss Arjun and Rani's story,
Marriage by Arrangement,
and more Nights at the Mahal novels coming soon,
by Sophia Singh Sasson.

Available from Harlequin Desire.

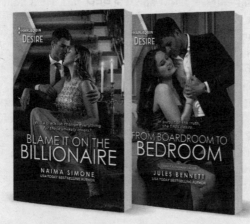

#2785 BACK IN THE TEXAN'S BED

Texas Cattleman's Club: Heir Apparent • by Naima Simone
When Charlotte Jarrett returns to Royal, Texas, with a child, no one's more surprised than her ex-lover, oil heir Ross Edmond. Determined to claim his son, he entices her to move in with him. But can rekindled passion withstand the obstacles tearing them apart?

#2786 THE HEIR

Dynasties: Mesa Falls • by Joanne Rock
To learn the truth about the orphaned boy she's raising, Nicole Cruz takes a job at Mesa Falls Ranch. Co-owner Desmond Pierce has his own suspicions and vows to provide for them. But he didn't expect the complication of a red-hot attraction to Nicole...

#2787 SCANDALIZING THE CEO

Clashing Birthrights • by Yvonne Lindsay
Falsely accused of embezzlement, executive assistant Tami Wilson is forced into spying on her boss, CEO Keaton Richmond, to prove her innocence. But it isn't long until their professional relationship turns very personal. What happens when Keaton learns the truth...?

#2788 ONE NIGHT WITH CINDERELLA

by Niobia Bryant
Shy housekeeper Monica Darby has always had feelings for handsome chef and heir to his family's fortune Gabe Cress. But one unexpected night of passion and a surprise inheritance change everything. With meddling families and painful pasts, will they find their happily-ever-after?

#2789 SEDUCING HIS SECRET WIFE

Redhawk Reunion • by Robin Covington
A steamy tryst leads to a quickie Vegas wedding for notorious CEO playboy Justin Ling and his best friend's sister, Sarina Redhawk. Then, to please investors and their disapproving families, they continue a fake relationship. Are their feelings becoming all too real?

#2790 TWICE THE TEMPTATION

Red Dirt Royalty • by Silver James
After a hurricane traps storm chaser Brittany Owens with tempting Cooper Tate, tension transforms into passion. But Cooper turns out to be her new boss! As their paths keep crossing, can she keep her promise to remain professional, especially when she learns she's pregnant—with twins?

"Hopefully everyone will get home safe," she said.

Gabe took in her high cheekbones, the soft roundness of her jaw
and the tilt of her chin. The scent of something subtle but sweet
surrounded her. He forced his eyes away from her and cleared his
throat. "Hopefully," he agreed as he poured a small amount of
champagne into his flute.

"I'll leave you to celebrate," Monica said.

With a polite nod, Gabe took a sip of his drink and set the bottle
at his feet, trying to ignore the reasons why he was so aware of her.
Her scent. Her beauty. Even the gentle night winds shifting her
hair back from her face. Distance was best. Over the past week he
had fought to do just that to help his sudden awareness of her ebb.
Ever since the veil to their desire had been removed, it had been
hard to ignore.

She turned to leave, but moments later a yelp escaped her as
her feet got twisted in the long length of her robe and sent her body
careening toward him as she tripped.

Reacting swiftly, he reached to wrap his arm around her waist
and brace her body up against his to prevent her fall. He let the hand
holding his flute drop to his side. Their faces were just precious

inches apart. When her eyes dropped to his mouth, he released a small gasp. His eyes scanned her face before locking with hers.

He knew just fractions of a second had passed, but right then, with her in his arms and their eyes locked, it felt like an eternity. He wondered what it felt like for her. Was her heart pounding? Her pulse sprinting? Was she aroused? Did she feel that pull of desire?

He did.

With a tiny lick of her lips that was nearly his undoing, Monica raised her chin and kissed him. It was soft and sweet. And an invitation.

"Monica?" he asked, heady with desire, but his voice deep and soft as he sought clarity.

"Kiss me," she whispered against his lips, hunger in her voice.

"Shit," Gabe swore before he gave in to the temptation of her and dipped his head to press his mouth down upon hers.

And it was just a second more before her lips and her body softened against him as she opened her mouth and welcomed him with a heated gasp that seemed to echo around them. The first touch of his tongue to hers sent a jolt through his body, and he clutched her closer to him as her hands snaked up his arms and then his shoulders before clutching the lapels of his tux in her fists. He assumed she was holding on while giving in to a passion that was irresistible.

Monica was lost in it all. Blissfully.

The taste and feel of his mouth were everything she ever imagined.

Ever dreamed of.

Ever longed for.

Don't miss what happens next in
One Night with Cinderella
by nationally bestselling author Niobia Bryant!

Available February 2021 wherever
Harlequin Desire books and ebooks are sold.

Harlequin.com

SPECIAL EXCERPT FROM

HQN

Read on for a sneak peek at
No Holding Back,
book one in New York Times *bestselling author*
Lori Foster's exciting new contemporary romance
series, The McKenzies of Ridge Trail.

Available February 2021 from HQN Books!

Cade wanted to kick his own ass.

She'd been coming into the bar for months now. She hadn't yet given her name, but he knew it all the same. He made a point of knowing everyone in the bar, whether they were important to his operation or not.

Sterling Parson. Star for short.

Privately, he called her Trouble.

At a few inches shy of six feet, she walked with a self-possessed air that he recognized as more attitude than ability. She wore that swagger like a warning that all but shouted, "Back off."

The big rig she drove had *SP Trucking* emblazoned on the side, yet she was far from the usual trucker they got as customers.

The day she'd first walked in, heads had swiveled, eyes had widened and interest had perked—but after Cade swept his gaze around the room, everyone had gotten the message.

The lady was off-limits.

From the moment he'd first spotted Sterling, he'd sensed the emotional wounds she hid, knew she had secrets galore and understood she needed a place to rest.

She needed him.

Star didn't know that yet, but no problem. In his bar, in this shit neighborhood, he'd look out for her anyway—same as he did for anyone in need.

Moving to the window, he watched her leave. Her long stride carried her across the well-lit gravel lot, not in haste but with an excess of energy. He couldn't imagine her meandering. The woman knew one speed: full steam ahead.

She climbed into her rig with practiced ease. Head tipped back, she rested a moment before squaring her shoulders and firing the engine. She idled for a bit, then eased off the clutch and smoothly rolled out to the road. Cade watched until he couldn't see her taillights anymore.

Where she'd go, he didn't yet know—but he wanted to. He wanted to introduce himself, ask questions, maybe offer assistance.

Her preferences on that were obvious.

Except that tonight she'd watched him a little more.

Actually, she often noticed him, in a cautious, distrustful way. And she always came back.

Sometimes she'd sleep for an hour, sometimes longer. Tonight, she'd dozed for two hours before jerking awake in alarm.

A bad dream?

Or a bad memory?

If she kept to her usual pattern, she'd be back tomorrow night on her return trip. Maybe, just maybe, he'd find a chink in her armor. He glanced at the little table she always chose.

Tomorrow, he'd offer her something different.

Don't miss No Holding Back *by Lori Foster,
available February 2021,
wherever HQN books and ebooks are sold.*

HQNBooks.com

PHLFEXP0221